TORRIE

AND THE

DRAGON

CORRIE

AND THE

DRAGON

K.V. JOHANSEN

ILLUSTRATIONS BY
DEAN BLOOMFIELD

ROUSSAN
PUBLISHERS INC.
Specializing in YA and fiction for pre-teens

THE CANADA COUNCIL | LE CONSEIL DES ARTS
FOR THE ARTS | DU CANADA
SINCE 1957 | DEPUIS 1957

We acknowledge the support of the Canada Council for the Arts for
our publishing program.

All rights reserved.

http://www.magnet.ca/roussan

Legal deposit 2nd quarter 1997

National Library of Canada
Bibliothèque nationale du Québec

Canadian Cataloguing in Publication Data
Johansen, K.V. (Krista V.), 1968-
Torrie and the dragon
(Out of this world series)
ISBN 1-896184-24-3
I. Bloomfield, Dean II. Title III. Series
PS8569.O2676T67 1997 jC813'.54 C97-900349-0
PZ7.J618To 1997

Cover design by Dan Clark
Cover art and illustrations by Dean Bloomfield
Interior design by Jean Shepherd

Published simultaneously in Canada and the United States of America

Printed in Canada

2 3 4 5 6 7 8 9 MRQ 2 1 0 9 8 7

DEDICATION

for Mum
with thanks to Douglas Lochhead

Chapter One

IN WHICH A HERO BECOMES A PRISONER

*I*t was a warm, still, Midsummer's night in the Wild
Forest. Beneath the full moon the entire Forest shimmered with shadows and moonlight, each leaf either silver or dark, and fluttering only when some small crea-
ture drifted past, moving softly as the wind might have.
But it was not a windy night.

If any humanfolk had been travelling through the Wild
Forest that night, they might have seen a strange sight, but
humans did not often travel across the mountains into the
Forest, and so only the animals that lived there saw the

huge bonfire on the rocky hilltop, and the peculiar crea-
tures sitting around it. And the animals did not think it
strange, for at least one night in every month the Old
Things of the Forest, and any that chanced to be passing
through, gathered to sing and dance and tell stories on this
high hilltop.

The Old Things were not animals, but neither were they
humans. They were Old, and they lived in the trees and
the rocks and the mountains and the waters; they always
had and they always would. Some of the creatures around
the bonfire were small and furry, others were large and
lumpy. There were tall, swaying tree-spirits called dryads,
and nymphs decked in waterweeds. Other beings were
spotted and speckled and blotched, winged or scaled or
fanged. Some were unbelievably beautiful, others just
plain hideously ugly, but they all sat and talked and
laughed together around the wildly twisting flames.

"Will you tell us a story, Torrie?" asked a squat, pur-
plish toad-thing. "Please?"

The other creatures sitting around the blue and orange
and scarlet fire whistled and clapped their paws and claws
and feet and branching fingers.

"Yes, Torrie, tell us a story!"

"A long story. One that'll last 'til sunrise."

"An adventure," cried some, and, "No, a love story!"
begged others.

"Tell us a fairy tale," said the deer-footed imp, "About
humans."

"Yes, Torrie! A fairy tale!"

Torrie got up off his rock, stood on it, and bowed. He was perhaps three feet tall, with long, slender fingers and toes. His eyes were large and golden, his ears were large and pointed, his nose was merely large. All over, he was covered in shaggy rust-coloured fur, and in his hand he carried a bronze-headed spear.

"A story," he said thoughtfully. "About humans?"

"Yes," said the toad. "You're always saying you know such a lot about them. So tell us!"

Torrie looked around at the circle of creatures, all eagerly leaning forward to hear what he might say. He grinned happily. His teeth were little and pointed.

"Very well," he said. "A story about humans, with adventures and love, to last until dawn."

He sat down again, and poked the fire with his spear. The creatures sighed happily, and leaned back against trees and stones, or sprawled beside the fire. The little clearing on top of the hill was quiet, save for the soft chatter of the leaves and the fire's sighs and snaps. Torrie spoke in the silence, and more shadows, the deer and foxes and rabbits of the Forest, crept from between the trees to listen as well.

"There are many different kinds of mortal men and women," Torrie began. "There are Philosophers and Madmen and Poets, and Craftsmen and Scientists and Scholars. And there are Heroes.

"I once knew a Hero, who was on a Quest. He met a

Beautiful Maiden, who was a particular friend of mine, and in the end they lived Happily-Ever-After, as is said to happen in human stories, although it rarely does. The Hero's name was Rufik, and he was the Crown Prince of the kingdom of Erythroth. The Maiden's name was Cossypha, and she was a Sorceress. Although it was not conventional at that time for Maidens to be Heroes (they were only supposed to marry them), she was as great a Hero as Rufik, and joined him on his Quest.

"Let me tell you their story."

It begins, as all good tales must, with the Hero beset by danger on all sides, surrounded by enemies thirsting for his blood. As was only natural, I suppose, for these enemies were wolves, and they looked hungry.

Rufik gripped his sword in a suddenly sweaty hand and glanced carefully over his shoulder. There were wolves behind him too, big, grey wolves, with gleaming eyes and teeth. They sat around his horse's feet and stood on the rocks overhanging the road and stared down at him, licking their chops. The wolves in the road ahead dangled pink tongues over dagger-like teeth, and grinned. The Prince's mare nickered uneasily and pawed the ground. Rufik patted her neck.

"I know, Banner, I know. I don't like them either," he said soothingly. He felt very un-soothed himself. What a way for his Quest to end. And he had barely

begun. Supper for a pack of wolves!

There were wolves in front and behind and on the steep slopes above the road, no escape anywhere. Rufik prepared himself to leap the good bay mare over their heads. Poor Banner couldn't possibly outrun so many, but as a prince and a hero, Rufik was honour-bound to try.

Someone, somewhere, whistled, and the wolves blocking his road moved back to the sides like a grey sea parting. The ones behind nipped at Banner's heels. She flattened her ears back to her skull, but she stayed still until Rufik's command to move forward between the ranks of laughing pink tongues. These, thought Rufik to himself, were not ordinary wolves, and he did not like it, not one bit. But he didn't seem to have much choice.

The wolves herded him like dogs herding sheep, although usually the sheep outnumber the dogs. Up a rise they went, and down into a gully and up and around a turn, along the edge of a cliff where the mountainside fell away, down, down, down below to a foaming river, and there was room for only one wolf on each side of the horse. Then up between rocks again, around another turn. Rufik pulled Banner up short.

There were three riders waiting for him, three riders like no men Rufik had ever seen before. They wore heavy black cloaks with the hoods pulled far forward, but in the shadows where faces should have been the

Prince could see the long grey muzzles of wolves, and under the hoods were the lumps of pricked-up wolf ears. The horses they rode were beautiful, shiny blue-black like beetles, but each had a set of wicked-looking horns that would have suited a champion yoke of oxen.

Brave horse though she was, this was too much for Banner, and she reared, whinnying in terror. Two of the wolf men grabbed her bridle and before Rufik could do anything, the third had wrested his sword from his grasp and had him on the ground. The last thing the Prince saw before a blow on the head knocked him senseless was the grinning teeth of a wolf man leaning over him, and the wolf had blue, human eyes.

"Wolves don't have blue eyes," said the deer-footed imp. "Their eyes are yellow, aren't they?"

"I don't know," said a water nymph. "We could look. Are there any wolves here tonight?"

The rabbits and deer looked around nervously. No wolves, just a few foxes.

"The point is," said Torrie, "that the wolf didn't have yellow eyes. Pay attention."

"I was paying attention. Why did it have blue eyes?"

"If you let me go on, you might find out," said Torrie. "Can I go on?"

Chapter Two

In which the Prisoner meets the Enchantress

When Rufik awoke he was being dragged down a staircase by the wolf men. Their claws dug into his armpits, and he could see his boots following him, bump, bump, bump, down the stairs. His feet, though, seemed too far away to really worry about much, considering how badly his head and his stomach ached. He sincerely hoped the Wolf men wouldn't drop him.

"What have you got there?" asked a voice from nowhere, a clear, musical voice utterly out of place in this nightmare of Wolf men and horned horses.

The Prince forced his dizzy eyes back up the stairs. There, silhouetted in the light of the doorway, was a slender, blurry figure, waving a stick at him. Rufik blinked, and the figure turned into a girl, a Maiden with hair the colour of copper coiled into a coronet about her head. She was dressed like one of the Royal Huntsmen, in a leather jerkin and leggings, and was holding a bow. Rufik stared.

"What have you caught?" she asked again.

"A prisoner, Milady," one of the wolf men growled, and hoisted Rufik up higher so the girl could have a better look. Rufik groaned; his head lolled to one side and he was sure he looked absolutely silly and very unheroic.

"I can see that, idiot," said the girl. "What kind of a prisoner? Who is he? Where did you find him?"

"A trespasser. The wolves caught him riding through the pass."

"Oh. Why would he do a thing like that?" asked the Maiden. "You, Trespasser! Don't you know that all this region of the mountains is ruled by Lord Sporryl the Enchanter? And he hates trespassers!"

Rufik tried to explain that he was only passing through on a Quest, but all he could say was "Urrr."

"He doesn't seem to be very bright, does he?"

"Well," mumbled the guard, rather embarrassed, "we sort of had to hit him over the head, your Ladyship. Probably knocked all the sense out of him."

"Oh. Still, he can't be too bright, to come riding into our mountains."

"That's true," said the wolf guard, and shook Rufik. "May we lock him up now, Milady?"

"Yes, yes," said the girl. "Don't keep him hanging there."

She ran lightly out the door and disappeared. Rufik moaned as he was hauled further down into the dungeon, bump, bump, bump.

The Beautiful Maiden, who is of course the Heroine of this story, was called Cossypha, as you would know if you'd been listening earlier, and she ran up the stairs in the castle, up and up and around and around, until she came to the topmost tower and her bedchamber.

"Torrie!" she called, once the door was safely shut behind her. "Torrie, where are you?"

I was up on the steep, slate roof of the tower, enjoying the last of the evening sun, but when I heard Cossypha calling I swung down and sat on the window sill.

I had been living in the castle of Sporryl the Enchanter for over a year then. Not because I liked Sporryl, who was the worst sort of dark magician, but because I liked his daughter, Cossypha, and she wasn't allowed to have any friends. They lived all alone in that big, drafty castle up in the mountains—the Enchanter and his daughter and the wolf guards, and me. The

Enchanter didn't know about me, of course. Humanfolk can see us only if we want them too, although some of you may have forgotten that; it's been so long since you've seen any. If Sporryl had ever caught me he would probably have used me for some evil enchantment or other. He was always doing things like that.

"I just got back from hunting goblins," said Cossypha, hanging her quiver of arrows on the hat stand with her sword and leaning her bow against it.

Among the creatures in the Forest listening to the tale, someone suddenly squawked.

"Hey," said Bobbin the goblin. "I don't like this story!"

"Shh," said an imp.

"Make her be hunting imps, Torrie," said the goblin.

"I can't," said Torrie. "It's a true story, and it was goblins. The mountains were full of goblin tribes, and they were all nasty, dirty, evil creatures. It's not my fault. They probably weren't any relations of yours. Now be quiet."

Bobbin was quiet, but she sulked.

"I was coming in from the stable, and guess what I saw!" said Cossypha. "There's a man in the dungeon, Torrie!"

"That's what your father uses his dungeon for," I said, "to put men in, men and other things."

"Yes, but it's been empty for years, because no one's such a fool as to try and cross the mountains on this pass anymore. This man was riding through the pass, and the wolves caught him."

"Oh." I considered this carefully. "He must be a Hero then. Only a Hero would do something that dangerous."

"Or a fool. He's probably a fool," said Cossypha sadly.

"Why should you care?" I asked.

"Who said I care?" Cossypha answered. "Drat. I'm going to be late for supper."

"You haven't fallen in love with this man in the dungeon, have you, Cossy?" I asked, more curious than ever. I had never seen a human in love before, but I knew that it was supposed to make them act quite strangely.

"Of course not!" Cossypha said indignantly. "I've only seen him for half a minute, and he seemed pretty stunned then. I wouldn't do anything so silly!"

She changed into a pale green gown, unbound and brushed out her hair. It flowed down to her heels like a river of molten copper, as I once heard a poet say. The Enchanter used to keep a Court Poet, but one evening he got mad at the man and changed him into a wolf guard.

"Are you sure you're not in love?" I asked, just to be certain.

"Of course I'm sure!"

And Cossypha swirled out, slamming the door behind her.

"I think you're in love, Cossy!" I called after her, but she didn't answer.

A prisoner in the dungeon! This I had to see. I skipped down the umpteen flights of stairs, making rude faces at the wolf-headed guards, who of course couldn't see me. The prisoner was singing a sad love song.

"Alas, my love, my only joy, so fair, so far, so distant." He stopped, and sighed deeply.

I squirmed between the bars of the cell. The iron made my fur stand on end and my skin burn, like when you rub your nose on ice.

He, Rufik the Prince, jumped when he saw me. He was sitting hunched in a pile of old, dusty straw in the corner of the cell, looking groggy. You must understand that although in those days we had much more to do with mortal humans (they believed in us, we believed in them, and so forth), anyway, even then most humans were not used to seeing us.

"Hullo, human," I said, by way of opening a conversation. "What are you doing here?"

He scrambled to his feet, rubbing his temples.

"My head hurts, and I'm seeing things. Little furry men. I just have to stay calm and it'll go away. Stay calm, Rufik," he said to himself, and shut his eyes.

After a bit he opened them. I grinned at him, and he whimpered and fell down in his straw.

"Are you a Hero?" I asked eagerly. "Are you on a Quest? There aren't many Heroes around these days."

The man didn't answer. He put his hands over his eyes.

"Listen, Hero! I'm real, believe in me. Talk to me. Or you can just stay here until Sporryl the Enchanter turns you into something nasty. I do have better things to do with my time."

I turned as if about to leave.

"Wait!" called the Hero. "Please! Are you real?"

"I think I am," said I. "Are you?"

"Yes, of course," he answered crossly.

"Good," I said. "I never talk to people who aren't real. Who are you? What are you?"

"I am Rufik James Augustus," he said, "Crown Prince of Erythroth. Who or what are you?"

"Torrie," I said. "I am Torrie, and Torrie means me. It rhymes with 'story'." I cackled, quite liking my little rhyme.

Rufik shuddered.

"So, Rufik James Augustus, Crown Prince of Erythroth, what were you doing, trying to cross the mountains along this pass? Sporryl the Enchanter doesn't like trespassers."

"So they keep telling me," said Rufik. "I was on my way to the Wild Forest on the other side, of course. I am on a desperate Quest, and time is of the utmost." He said this last quite grandly. I was impressed.

"Of the utmost what?" I asked.

He blinked in confusion.

"Of the utmost importance, I think. My father's kingdom of Erythroth is in grave danger, you see. There's a dragon laying waste to it."

"Ahh," I said wisely. "And you're fleeing across the mountains to safety."

"I'm doing no such thing!" Rufik shouted. "I'm on a Quest! I have to find a Magic Sword, the Wormbane, and kill the Dragon and save the kingdom. The Sword Wormbane is supposed to be hidden somewhere in the Wild Forest, until the Hero claims it to save his kingdom. According to an old, old book in the library, anyway. I don't know, I've been questing for a week, and I haven't found out anything more about this Magic Sword yet."

"Well, you've barely started," I said. "You haven't even got to the Wild Forest yet."

"It doesn't look like I'm going to, either," muttered the Prince.

"I could let you out," I said.

"Could you, Torrie?" he cried, and jumped to his feet. "That would be marvelous. But..." and he sat back down again.

"But what?"

"How can I go off on a Quest, and leave my heart

here?"

"What?" I said. His heart seemed to be in his chest where it was supposed to be. Sporryl hadn't done anything to him yet. Then I became suspicious.

"You're not in love, are you?"

"I'm afraid so," said Rufik gloomily. "Probably the worst thing that ever happened to me. What am I supposed to do now?"

"Finish the Quest and marry the girl, that's how it happens."

"But how can I? I don't even know her name, and she dwells here with my enemy, the Enchanter!"

I patted his knee. "There, there, Rufik. Things will work out. Tell me, what is she like, this love of yours?"

As if I didn't know.

Rufik sighed, rustling the cobwebs in the corners.

"She is as beautiful as a sunset over the sea. Her hair is red gold, her voice like the lark in the morning."

Rufik sighed again.

"Red hair. You mean Cossypha, Sporryl's daughter. She's a great Enchantress herself."

"You know her?" cried Rufik, leaping to his feet again. "Could you, would you take her a message?"

I'd always known something interesting would happen to Cossy someday, and here was a Hero on a Quest, ready to die of a broken heart for her sake. Fun, fun, fun! I wriggled out between the bars.

"You stay here, Rufik, I'll be back!"

"Wait!" he called. "Torrie, wait!"
But I was already halfway upstairs.

I stopped by the dining hall and peeked around the door. There was a long, long table that could seat fifty guests. Sporryl sat at the head, Cossypha at the foot. There were spider webs and dust on all the chairs in between. Evil Enchanters do not have many dinner guests. They were waited on by the Wolf men, and Sporryl's favourite wolf lay at his feet. It growled at me. I growled back. Cossypha frowned. She was afraid that someday her father would find out what the wolves kept growling at. And then he would do something nasty to me. I winked at her and wiggled my ears, and skipped off to her tower.

"What's wrong with you, have you got fleas or something?" asked Cossypha as soon as she escaped from the dreary dinner. I was still dancing around the room, giggling.
"Fleas!" I shrieked. "Ha! Here I go and solve all your problems, go all the way down to the dungeon, go crawling through all those iron bars…I shall probably get a rash! And you say I have fleas! Hmmph. You can just go talk to your Hero yourself!"
I sat on the window sill, pretending to look out at the pink sunset clouds.

"You talked to the prisoner?" said Cossypha. "What did he say? Why did he come here? Who is he?"

"Go away. I'm not talking to you."

"Torrie!" she pleaded.

"I'm not."

"I'll push you off," she said.

"You wouldn't."

"Yes I would."

"No you wouldn't."

"I would, you know."

"I know you wouldn't."

"I thought you weren't talking to me," said Cossypha in triumph. I bit my tongue and didn't answer.

"I'll tickle you!"

"You wouldn't! No, Cossy! Don't! Please! I'll talk! I'll talk! Stop!"

We chased around the room, shrieking, until we both collapsed panting on the hearth rug.

"Did you really talk to the prisoner?" Cossypha asked.

"You said I had fleas," I reminded her.

She sighed. "All right, all right, you don't have fleas. Anyway, you made me tie my hair all in knots."

"Do you really want to hear about the prisoner?" I asked.

"No, not really," said Cossypha carelessly. "But you can tell me if you want." She got up and began looking for a comb.

"Well, if you don't care," I shrugged. "I'm going to go talk to the horses. They're better company."

"No!" Cossypha dropped her comb. "Drat. Torrie, tell me, please."

"Okay." I bounced onto her bed. "His name is Rufik something something, Crown Prince of Erythroth. He's a Hero on a Quest for a Magic Sword called Wormbane, to kill a dragon and save his kingdom."

"Oh, is that all?"

"Is that all? Real live Heroes are scarce these days. And here's one in your dungeon, pining for you."

"He's not!" said Cossypha. "We haven't even been introduced."

"Yes, he is too pining for you. Come and I'll introduce you, and then we can escape with him."

"I'm not escaping with some man I don't know!" said Cossypha. "It's not ladylike."

"Well, hunting goblins isn't ladylike," I said. "Not that I know any ladies other than you. Besides, he's an honourable sort of Hero."

Bobbin the goblin hissed. "You don't know what you're talking about, Torrie. Your Cossy never met a real goblin, I bet. A real goblin would have eaten her. So there."

"Shut up, Bobbin!" said the purple toad-thing.

"We could escape on our own," said Cossypha. "I've

thought about it a lot. But then poor Father would be so lonely."

"He has the wolf guards," I said. "You know he never talks to you anyway, aside from your magic lessons. You have to have a life of your own, Cossy. Anyhow, it'll be more fun escaping with Rufik. We'll get to see a dragon. And besides, he needs our help. He's not very good at being a Hero; he's only been doing it for a week and he's already got himself captured. So we have to help him. And you don't want to break his heart."

"His heart is in no danger of breaking, Torrie," said Cossypha, stamping her foot. "Stop saying that. You stay here and I'll go talk to your Hero."

"He's not my Hero," I muttered. "I don't want him."

Chapter Three

In which we rescue the Prisoner

I gave Cossypha a five-minute head start, then followed her down to the dungeon. The wolf guards were asleep at their posts. I wasn't lying when I told the Prince that Cossy was a great Enchantress. I tied the wolf men's whiskers in knots before scampering to the cell to climb up Cossypha's hair and perch on her shoulder.

"When are we leaving?" I asked.

"Be quiet, Torrie," ordered Cossypha. "I thought I told you to stay upstairs."

"I didn't hear you."

Cossypha ignored me and turned back to Rufik.

"But you don't even know where this Magic Sword is! How on earth are you supposed to find it?"

"Luck, I guess," said Rufik. "Or fate? I shall just wander until I get a sign. That's what happens in the tales. Some kindly fairy or mysterious old man will set me on my way."

"Rufik," said Cossypha. "The Wild Forest is huge. No one has ever reached its borders. You could wander for the rest of your life in it without finding a kindly fairy or a mysterious old man, let alone the Sword Wormbane. You'll get eaten by bears or goblins or trolls or something. Couldn't you kill the Dragon with an ordinary sword?"

"I don't think that would work," said Rufik glumly. "It is a dragon, after all."

"I suppose so" sighed Cossypha. "Well, you certainly need help, you'll never manage on your own."

"Whoo-heee!" I yelled. "We're going on a Quest!"

"Don't swing on my hair, Torrie!" Cossypha yelled.

"Shh! pleaded Rufik. "The guards will hear."

"The guards won't hear a thing until dawn," said Cossy.

"I told you she was an Enchantress," I said.

Cossypha frowned at me. "Torrie, you go harness the horses. We'll meet in the stable."

"Wait," called Rufik. "Where are you going?"

Cossypha turned back. "I'm going to change my clothes, of course. Surely you don't expect me to go off Questing dressed like this!"

"It's very beautiful," said Rufik humbly, and blushed.

Cossypha sniffed and gathered her trailing green skirts up in one hand.

"It may be," she said, "but it is not practical."

She tossed her long, flowing hair back over her shoulder, like a cloak of flame (there, isn't that poetic?) and ran lightly up the stairs.

Rufik sighed.

"Stop that," I said, straightening my whiskers, and chased after Cossypha. I caught her halfway up the stairs.

"Cossy!"

"Let go of my hair!"

"Sorry. You see? Isn't it marvelous, he's a handsome Hero on a Quest. Aren't you glad I told you about him?"

"I told *you* about him! And he isn't all that handsome."

"Oh. Isn't he? I thought Heroes always were. Is he terribly ugly then?"

It would be so sad if Cossypha ran away with an ugly Hero. We'd have to wait for another one, or run away on our own. But there's not much point to just running away, we needed a Quest or something to keep us amused.

"No!" said Cossy. "He's not ugly!"

"Oh, good."

"Torrie, go harness the horses. And see if you can find Prince Rufik's sword. He'll probably need it before we find Wormbane."

"You and I can look after him."

"Torrie!"

"I'm going!"

It was nice to know Rufik was a proper handsome Hero, or at least not ugly. You never can tell with mortals. They might think curling cinnamon hair and a slightly freckled nose were terribly ugly. You never can tell.

I found Rufik's sword in the guardroom and dragged it by the belt into the stable. I hate the touch of steel. And of course all the harness buckles were iron. I was going to get a rash. Or blisters. Why didn't they use bronze or something nice?

Rufik's horse was a true lady. Her name was Banner, she said. She was quite willing to let me harness her, once I told her we were escaping with her master. It was an awkward task, even with her cooperation, because the saddle weighed nearly as much as I did. But I got it done in the end. I'm very strong, you know.

Cossypha's steed, though, was one of Sporryl's blue-black, horned beasts like the wolf men rode. He was young and excitable, and I nearly got trampled. His

name was Darby. He never had liked me much.

Cossypha arrived just as I had finished and was sitting on Banner's back sucking my iron-burned fingers.

"Oh Torrie, I forgot," she cried. "Your poor hands!"

"They're all right," I said, not whimpering the slightest. "Are you ready?"

"Hey!" said Bobbin. "You've forgotten about—"

"Shh!" said the purple toad-thing.

"I asked Cossypha, ARE YOU READY?" said Torrie loudly.

"I think so," she said. She had dressed in her goblin-hunting clothes again, and her hair was bound up out of the way, probably so I couldn't climb on it. She fastened a pack behind Darby's saddle. "Where's what's-his-name? Rufik?"

"I thought you were getting him," said I.

"I thought you were."

I sighed and started to climb down. "Humans. I'll go get him."

"I'll go," said Cossypha, and went.

"The Enchanter will come after us," said Darby, rubbing his horns on a post. "Good thing I'm the fastest horse in the stable. But her, can she keep the pace?"

Banner's ears went back.

"We'll see who slows down whom, youngster!"

"Easy, easy," I interrupted, not wanting to be in the middle of a horse fight.

Banner turned her head, muttering something that sounded like "common cattle". The other horned horses whispered and snickered. They felt young Darby needed taking down a bit. He boasted too often about goblin hunting with Cossy.

There were footsteps in the passageway from the castle. Cossypha and the Prince.

"Careful," said Cossy, "there's a step," as Rufik fell over it. He buckled on his sword and patted Banner happily.

"I hate dungeons," he told her.

Cossypha led the way and Rufik followed, never taking his eyes off her.

"I never thought," he whispered to me, "that I would appreciate a Maiden wearing trousers."

I still haven't figured out what he meant.

We rode as fast as we could through the twisting mountain pass, reaching the foothills as the rising sun flung flame along the cloudy horizon. Then we galloped along on a narrow track through the forest fragrant with pines and echoing with bird song. But it was dawn, and Cossypha's spell binding the wolf guards in sleep was ended. Sporryl would be after us.

"Good!" said Bobbin.

Chapter Four

IN WHICH THE WOLF GUARDS COME AFTER US

Red sky at night, sailors delight,
Red sky in the morning, sailors take warning.

That's what the humans say about a sunrise like the one which burned in the sky before us. Me, I didn't need their little rhyme to tell the weather, I could smell the thunder in the wind. The red dawn clouds faded to grey and the birds fell silent.

We didn't stop for breakfast, but ate apples and cheese and bread as we rode. Sensible Cossypha had re-membered food. I must confess that in the excitement of the moment I had forgotten all about it. After all, I could forage in the woods. Humanfolk are hopeless at such tasks though. They make so much noise that everything runs away; they walk on nests or under them and never notice; and as for plants, the poor things can't smell what's good and what's not, and are always poisoning themselves.

"I'm hungry," interrupted the red-eyed goblin suddenly.

Several of the smaller rabbits scurried away. The purple toad-thing sighed. "You shouldn't talk about food when Bobbin's here, Torrie. It always makes her hungry."

"Well, it's not my fault," the goblin sulked. "When I'm hungry, I'm hungry." Her stomach rumbled like distant thunder. "See?"

Another group of rabbits fled.

"Someone feed the goblin, quickly," muttered Torrie. "I can't tell a story with her complaining all the time."

"I'm not complaining," Bobbin protested. "I just said that—"

"Shh," hissed a hazel dryad. "Let Torrie tell his story."

"But I'm hungry!"

The dryad offered a double handful of nuts, and the toad groaned. "If you sit there crunching nuts all night, we'll never hear the end of this tale."

Torrie began to stomp around the fire, grumbling. "If nobody wants to hear the rest…"

"*Torrie, Torrie, tell!*"

"*She'll be quiet. Go on with the story!*"

"*Eat quietly, Bobbin.*"

The goblin grinned, a dreadful sight, and swallowed the hazel-nuts in one mouthful.

"*She didn't even shell them,*" *whispered the deer-footed imp in awe.*

"*Shhh!*"

"*Is everyone quite done snacking?*" *asked Torrie, sitting down again.* "*Can I go on?*"

"*And nobody else is to get hungry,*" *ordered the toad.* "*I want to hear the tale, not some goblin's stomach.*"

Bobbin giggled, and hiccoughed, and a nymph pounded her on the back.

"*SHHH!*"

Where was I! Oh yes.

By midmorning the sky was black and churning, and thunder grumbled along the tops of the mountains. We were in a dark valley, where the sound of the horses' hooves was muffled by close-growing oaks. We kept together and silent, it was that sort of place.

"I don't like it here," said Cossypha's horned horse. "I want to go home."

"You can't go home, Darby," I said. "We're on a Quest. You should be proud and bold and heroic."

Darby shook his horns. "I am proud and bold and heroic. But I don't like this place. It's spooky."

"Baby," I said.

Darby snorted, arched his neck and pranced a bit to show he wasn't really so frightened.

Rufik's horse, Banner, flicked an ear at me, laughing.

"I don't like this place," said Rufik.

"Don't you start!" I moaned.

"Start what?" asked the Prince in surprise.

"He's probably been talking to the horses," said Cossypha. "But you can't always believe they said what he said they did. I think he makes half of it up."

"Not half," I said. "Not nearly half. A quarter, maybe."

There was a crash of thunder and the rain suddenly poured down. I crawled under Rufik's cloak, but it didn't do much good; it was soaked through in minutes. When I finally stuck my head out again, we were in a rocky clearing at the top of a hill.

Far behind, I could see the way we had come, a track winding along the valley and up the hillside, looking now like a river of mud. There were dark shadows lurching along the mud. I rubbed rain and fur out of my eyes. Black cloaked riders on black horses, and every horse had horns.

"Run!" I yelled, leaping to Rufik's shoulder. "Run! The wolf guards are behind us!"

Rufik shrieked, I think perhaps he didn't like me yelling in his ear. We galloped along the slippery track, down the other side of the hill into the trees again. I clutched Rufik's belt as we splashed and squelched along the treacherous path, somehow avoiding the roots and rocks. Banner slipped in the mud once and almost fell. I leapt over to Darby, the mare recovered herself and we raced on.

The rain continued to pour, but not fast enough to hide our tracks. Down we went, and at the bottom of the hill we hit a shallow, pebbly river in a great burst of spray, which at least washed off the mud.

"Stop! Stop!" I cried at the top of my lungs. "Whoah! Halt!"

The horses heard and whoa-ed, sidling around in the middle of the river with water foaming against their bellies.

"Torrie!" Cossypha shouted above the noise of the river and the rain. "What are you doing? They'll catch us!"

"They'll catch us anyhow, if we keep charging along in the mud. All we need is for one of the horses to fall, and the wolf guards can overtake us. We need to be clever."

"Standing in the middle of a river getting soaked and waiting for the guards is clever?" asked Cossypha. "I never realized it. We might just as well have never left!"

Rufik drew his sword.

"Torrie is right. We must prepare an ambush. String your bow, Lady Cossypha."

"We can't fight them," said Cossypha in horror, and

I said, "No, no, NO, Rufik! This is not the time to be heroic."

"I know we are outnumbered," said the Prince. "But it is our only chance."

"You don't understand," Cossypha said. "Rufik, we can't fight the wolf-headed guards, they're people just like you. Travellers through the mountains. Adventurers and minstrels and salesmen, and the Cook and the Court Poet. My father enchanted them, like he was going to do to you."

"Oh," said Rufik, and again, "Oh!" He turned pale. "But what else can we do?"

"If you two would let me speak," I said. "I have a plan."

"You have plans about everything," said Cossypha. "They never work."

"Yes they do."

"No they don't. Remember the time you wanted to capture the king of the goblins? That didn't work, we almost got killed!"

"Good!" said Bobbin. "It's about time! Three cheers for the goblins! I wish they had killed your Sorceress, then I wouldn't have to listen to this stupid story."

"Shut up!" said the purple toad-thing.

"It'd be different if it was toads," said Bobbin, and stuck out her tongue.

"Bobbin!" shouted a chorus of nymphs, and the goblin

was so startled she was quiet.

"Thank you," said Torrie, and continued.

"That doesn't count," I said. "And we didn't get killed, anyhow. Now come on, we don't have much time. Down the river. That'll confuse them. Being turned partly into wolves, their heads are all fuzzy and they can't think very well."

"They can see us just fine though," said Cossypha. "Look!"

True, while we argued the wolf-headed guards had mounted the crest of the hill and were now riding down the slope toward us, pointing and waving swords. One horse slipped and fell and another tripped over it. For a moment they looked like a big, black, four-horned spider, waving eight legs out of the mud, while their two wolf-headed riders ran around them and snapped at one another.

"Gee up!" I yelled in Darby's big hairy ear, and he jumped, almost throwing both Cossypha and me into the river.

"Torrie!" she yelled. "Stop doing that!"

"I can't hear you," I said. "My ears are full of water."

Well, they were.

With the water so deep, the horses couldn't really run, so they lurched along, stumbling across to the other bank, and we splashed as fast as we could through the shallows. We could hear the wolf guards shouting and howling behind us. They hadn't reached the river yet.

"Look!" I said. "Cossy, turn here."

"What?" she said.

There was a tiny stream bubbling out from under the low-growing trees to join the river. You could hardly see it between the steep, bush-covered banks.

"If we go up here," I said patiently, "the guards won't see us, and they'll think we've gone down the river. They'll go tearing along past us, and get tired and give up and go home."

I started to giggle. It was such a wonderful plan.

Rufik frowned. "I don't think *I* could crawl up that brook, let alone the horses."

"Of course they can," I said indignantly. He wasn't going to spoil my plan. "They'll just have to keep their heads down."

"Tell the horses that if they leave any tracks on the bank, or break any branches that the guards can see, I'll feed them to the wolves," said Cossypha severely. "Come on then. Rufik, you go first."

"She didn't mean that, did she?" asked Darby. "She wouldn't feed me to the wolves, would she, Torrie?"

"Don't be silly," I told him. "She'd feed you to the wolf *guards*."

I winked at Banner, who winked back. Poor Darby had no sense of humour.

The humans had to duck as they led the horses

under the overhanging branches. The horses stretched out their necks and tiptoed. Darby tried to suck in his sides. Soon they had all disappeared from sight into the green darkness. Even the sound of their splashing was lost in the rain and the river.

I stayed at the mouth of the brook to watch for the wolf guards. Soon they came by, riding much more cautiously than we had, and looking wet and miserable.

"They've gone," said one.

"Gone entirely," said another.

"Well, we'll never catch up with them now," said a third, and they all nodded.

"Besides, the Lady is an Enchantress," said a fourth. "Turned them all invisible, she has. Probably hiding right here laughing at us."

I couldn't stop it, a laugh burst out, but it too got lost in the rain.

"Let's go home," said the wolf guard captain, who had once been the Court Poet. "We've tried."

And they all turned their horses around. Two got their horns entangled and had a tug of war in the river until one rider fell off and I had to laugh again. Finally they were all pointing the right direction, riding dejectedly back up the river toward the mountains.

I waded up the little brook after my humans and their horses. They were making a camp under some trees, and the Prince was having no luck starting a fire with the wet wood.

"Why are we stopping?" I asked. "It's not supper time yet."

"Because we're wet," said Rufik. "My boots are squishing, my socks are dripping, and I don't even have any dry underwear in my pack. Everything's soaked. We need to make a fire and dry out."

"I can live with wet clothes," said Cossypha. "But we need to make a plan. We can't just wander forever hoping to trip over this magic dragon-killing Sword."

"Wormbane, it's called," interrupted Rufik.

"We can't just wander around waiting to trip over Wormbane. We need a search plan, or we'll be lost in the Wild Forest forever. So we might as well stop now and think about where we're going, and dry out while we do it."

"You won't get dry until it stops raining," I said. "And I already have a plan for finding the Magic Sword."

"I'll bet," said Cossypha.

"Well, I do."

"Tell me, then."

"We wander through the Wild Forest and look for clues, and then we find the Sword, go back to the kingdom of Erythroth, and kill the Dragon."

"Torrie, that is not a plan."

"I don't know," said Rufik. "It sounds like a good plan to me."

"I'm glad I'm Questing with two such wonderful planners," muttered Cossypha to herself. "I'm going to look for dry wood."

She didn't find any, but I did, up under the thickly needled branches of a giant spruce tree. Spruce trees are always filled with little dead twigs, good for starting fires. But there was no larger wood dry enough to burn afterwards. Cossypha dragged back a big fallen branch, found a hatchet and started to chop it into shorter lengths. Rufik and I watched her. Rufik had draped all the wet clothes from his pack over my little pile of dry twigs, trying to keep the rain off it.

"That's not going to burn, Milady," said Rufik helpfully. "It's too wet."

"It will burn just fine," said Cossypha, tucking wet wisps of hair behind her ears. "I know what I'm doing."

"I don't," I said. "But I found some dry kindling."

"Good," said Cossypha.

She let Rufik take the hatchet and finish chopping, while she cleared away all the plants from a muddy circle, and put my little pile of twigs in the middle of it, with some larger, wet logs leaning over them.

"Now," she said, and glared at the wood. "I just hope I can remember this."

She waved her hands over it three times, whispering something. I crept closer to hear what she was saying. Cossypha stopped and sat back on her heels.

"Torrie, if you don't move further away, I'll set your ears on fire by mistake."

I scuttled away behind Rufik, and Cossy started her spell again. First the little twigs began to smoke a bit, then there was a *whooosh* sort of noise, and all the wet logs were burning cheerfully. The flame was a pale lavender colour, but warm for all that.

Rufik said nothing, but his eyes were very round. After a while he built a frame out of thin saplings and they hung the wet clothes from their packs on it to dry, and it was supper time.

"Rain is the best weather to fish in," said the Prince, and he found some fishhooks and line in a little pouch, tied them to a stick, and went to look for worms. Cossypha and I sat wrapped up in a soggy blanket, watching the rain sizzling in the air just before it hit the fire. Nothing was dry, but it was very cozy. By the time Rufik came back with six little speckled trout the rain had finally stopped, and my fur was starting to feel fluffy again.

Cossypha didn't mention plans again that night. After all, we were in the middle of a vast uninhabited forest. There was no one to ask for directions and we had no idea which way the Sword lay. Wandering aimlessly would work as well as anything else, even Cossypha could see that, and besides, all true Heroes have luck on their side. And I believed Rufik was a true Hero, even if Cossypha wasn't sure yet.

CHAPTER FIVE

IN WHICH WE FIND A BURIED BEAR

We travelled north, away from the mountains, for several days, following little paths that meandered through the trees and faded away to nothing. The land here was still very hilly, with great piles of rock pushing out of the earth in places, and trees trying to grow on top of the rocks.

"When does the bear come into it?" asked the deer-footed imp.

"What bear?" asked Torrie.

"You said you met a bear, but you haven't yet."

"I hope it eats that silly goblin-killer," said Bobbin.

"If I haven't told you about the bear yet," said Torrie, "it is because it is not yet time to tell you about the bear. If you want to finish the story yourself you may. I'm going to leave and go fishing."

"No, no," said the imp. "I'm sorry, Torrie. Go on."

Torrie coughed and went on.

We didn't see any animals other than foxes and deer and rabbits, but it felt like the kind of place a bear, or a dozen bears, might live, so we always built a great fire at night. One evening we heard wolves howling, and the humans and horses were frightened, even though Cossypha was used to wolves. These were very civil wolves, though, not like Sporryl's flea-ridden, ill-mannered, surly pack, and I went off to speak to them while the humans were trying to sleep. The wolves had never heard of a Magic Sword anywhere in the Wild Forest, and they were not very interested in dragons or heroes. They promised not to chase my humans or their horses, though.

We kept riding north, for lack of a better direction. One day, about a week after we had escaped from Sporryl, the horses and I heard whimpering as we rode along the crest of a jagged, rocky hill.

"What's that?" asked Banner, cocking an ear.

Darby tilted his head on one side, so that a horn nearly touched the ground. I jumped down and put my ear against the hill.

"Woe, woe, woe," I heard, each "woe" a faint, long echo. "Oh woe. The dark is dark, the black is black, no more will sunlight shine on my back. Oh woe." And someone snuffled mightily.

"What is it?" asked Rufik. "Why have we stopped?"

"It's a bad poet," I said, with my ear still to the ground. "The hill is singing very bad poetry to itself."

"That's not the hill," said Banner. "That's someone inside the hill."

Darby stamped his hoof on the earth. The snuffling stopped.

"Hullo?" asked the hill hesitantly. "Is anyone out there? Up there? Or there at all? Probably not. I'm just going mad.

> Oh woe is me, I'm going mad,
> A mournful bear,
> I'm very sad,
> I'll never see the sun again,
> I'll never see the sparkling rain..."

"Hullo!" I said, speaking right into the earth. "Your poetry is terrible, Bear."

There was a long, long silence.

"Your poetry would probably be terrible, too," said the voice inside the hill, "if you were trapped in a cave with rocks on you. Who are you?"

"Torrie," I said.

"Are you a giant, Torrie?" asked the bear.

"No," I said. "I'm just Torrie. Why do you want a giant?"

"To move the rocks and get me out," said the bear. "Oh woe. I'm very hungry. The roof fell down in my cave during a thunderstorm. Rocks fell on one of my hind legs, and it's broken, and there's no light anymore, the tunnel is filled with rocks. Woe, woe, woe."

"I have a Sorceress and a Hero with me, though," I told the bear, after thinking a minute. "If you promise not to eat them, or their horses, or me, we'll try to get you out."

The bear said nothing, and I could hear it snuffling. It was weeping for joy.

"What are you doing?" asked Cossypha.

"Talking to a bear," I said, and I told the humans about the bear.

"Poor thing," she said. "Of course we'll try to rescue it."

"What if it wants to eat us?" asked Rufik cautiously.

"It's a polite bear," I said. "It's highly unlikely to eat its benefactors. But first we have to think of a way to rescue it."

"We could begin by finding the tunnel that collapsed," said Cossypha.

So we started searching the hill. It was a very large hill, and it took a very long time to find the entrance to the bear's cave.

"I've found it!" called Rufik after an hour or so. "Look here, everyone."

We all came and looked. There was a path winding up the rockiest side of the hill. Halfway up it disappeared into some honeysuckle bushes, and when you crawled into them, you found a dark crack between two huge slabs of stone. If you crept between the rocks, you were in a tunnel, its earth walls rubbed smooth by the passing of the bear. But after a few yards, there was no more tunnel, just a heap of wet mud and stones, where the roof had fallen down. Rufik poked at the tumble with his sword.

"I don't think it's very thick," he decided. "We should be able to dig it out."

He pulled at a small stone. It came out all right, but more slid down to take its place.

"Oh dear," said Rufik.

"I think I know a spell that might help," said Cossypha. "It's for levitating things."

"For what?" asked Rufik.

"Levitating things," I said. "You know. Explain to him, Cossy."

Cossypha gave me a look and said, "Why don't you explain, Torrie?"

"Because you can do it better," I told her, and stuck out my tongue.

"Levitation means making things float," Cossypha explained. "For example, I could pick Torrie here up off the ground without touching him."

"No you couldn't," I said hastily. The two humans had to crawl on their hands and knees through most of the tunnel; the roof wasn't very high. But in the pale grey light coming through the honeysuckle, Cossypha was drawing circles in the air and chanting in some strange language. (Humans often put their spells in ancient, forgotten languages, to keep them secret.)

My feet were leaving the ground. I tried to hang on with my toenails, but it did no good. Slowly, like a piece of dandelion fluff, I drifted up until I was lying on my back in the air, bobbing under the roof with my nose just brushing the rocks. I pushed myself away and shot down toward the floor, but I just bounced back to the ceiling. Rufik fell over on his back, laughing and holding his stomach.

"I like this bit," said Bobbin. "Let's find someone to levitate Torrie again, and he can float away."

Torrie pretended not to hear.

"Cossy!" I said pleadingly, and she stopped giggling and unlevitated me. I fell on Rufik.

"You see?" said Cossypha. "If I put a spell like that on the roof of the tunnel and the cave, it'll help hold it up until we get out. Now we just need something to dig with."

Surprisingly, Rufik had a small spade in his gear. He thought the Sword Wormbane might be buried somewhere. While he began to dig a way through the fallen debris, standing on his knees because of the low roof, Cossypha and I dragged the loads of mud and rocks out of the tunnel on slabs of bark from a dead elm tree. The horses grazed in the sun and did nothing. Several times Cossypha had to strengthen the spell supporting the roof, as more of it trembled and tried to fall, disturbed by Rufik's digging. There were a few stray levitated rocks floating on their own, drifting a little in the draft. Finally, Rufik broke through into the bear's den. There was a low, rumbling sound, and the Prince backed carefully into the tunnel again.

"Torrie," he whispered. "Torrie! You'd better do something. It growled at me."

"That wasn't a growl," I said. "That was saying hello. Can't you tell the difference?"

I squeezed past him into the cave.

"Hullo Bear."

"So you're a Torrie," said the bear. "I've never met one before. But I've made a little song for you. It goes like this:

A bear lay in a darksome cave,
He thought it soon would be his grave;
But Torrie came with heroic friends,
And saved the bear from dismal ends.

It would sound a bit better if you had only one friend, then I could have said, from dismal end, but that's the way it is. Could you get these rocks off my leg, do you think?"

Cossypha and Rufik had now crept into the cave, too. It took both of them to lift the fallen rocks off the bear's right hind leg, but when they had done so it stood up on the other three, weak and wobbly from hunger, and dragged itself down the tunnel while we crawled behind, being encouraging. Once outside, the bear lay in the sun with its eyes shut, just smelling the grass and the honeysuckle. There was rumbling within the hill and all the rest of the cave and tunnel roof fell in. Cossypha had let go of her levitation spell.

The bear stretched asleep in the sun, while we all sat around in the grass and watched it.

"Can you fix its leg?" I asked Cossypha. She had her chin on her knees and was glaring at the bear's crooked leg like it was the bear's own fault for having broken it. But I knew she was just thinking hard.

"I don't know," she answered finally. "That's a lot harder than levitation spells. It's quite near the back of the book, and I hadn't gotten that far when we left."

"What book?" asked Rufik.

"Father's spell book."

"You should have stolen it," I said.

"That would have been wrong," said Rufik sternly. "Stealing me was different."

"Besides," said Cossypha. "He keeps it in the library, with a spell on it to make sure no one steals it."

"Could you try to fix the bear?"

"I could try," she said. "But I've only read the spell for Broken Bones and Infection once or twice, when I was just looking ahead. If I got something wrong, or forgot a word or a line, anything could happen. It might be better if we just put a splint on the leg and let it heal itself."

"It wouldn't be as much fun for the bear," I said.

"It wouldn't be much fun for the bear if I turned it into a hippopotamus either," said Cossypha.

"A hippo-what?" asked Rufik.

"-potamus. It's a large sort of animal that lives in rivers in the south. Sort of like a giant pig," I started to explain. "They frolic in the rivers all day, and eat things. Maybe the bear would like to be a hippopoppomus."

"-potamus," said Cossypha.

"I know. We could ask it."

"But it might get turned into a black fly, or a toadstool, or anything. Or it might go out poof like a candle. It's not safe to do spells that you can't remember."

"Well, try to remember," I said. "I'm going to find some food for me and the bear. It'll be hungry when it wakes up."

"Well, I hope it doesn't wake up until you get back, then," said Rufik.

"I wonder what a prince tastes like," said Bobbin the goblin, and her red eyes glittered. "Do you cook them with onions or cabbage?"

CHAPTER SIX

IN WHICH WE GET NEWS ABOUT THE SWORD AT LAST

When I came back with a bag full of mushrooms and part of an anthill, the bear was awake and making little whimpering noises while Rufik stroked its huge black head and said, "There, there, brave fellow, we'll soon set you right," and other heartening words. Cossypha was sitting on a rock at the top of the hill with her head in her hands.

"We set the bear's leg, and put a splint on it," said Rufik. "It howled, but it didn't try to bite us. I think it's a very sick bear."

"Of course it is," I said. "It's half-starved. What's wrong with Cossy?"

"She's trying to decide whether or not to use the healing spell," said the Prince, whispering so the bear couldn't hear. "She's still afraid of getting it wrong, but she thinks the bear's so sick it might die if she doesn't. I think she's crying, Torrie. What do I do?"

"Do about what?" I asked.

"Cossypha."

I considered. "Do you have to do anything?"

"Of course I do. She's unhappy. She needs me to comfort her."

"Usually I tickle her or hang her boots out the window or something," I said. "But I don't think that would be a good idea at the moment. I think that you should leave her alone and let her think. It's not *you* that might turn the bear into something awful like a goblin—"

"Shut up, Bobbin!"

"—like a goblin or a fungus."

Rufik sighed deeply and sat down on a rock where he could watch Cossypha, sitting thinking on her rock. Humans!

I laid out the mushrooms, lovely firm, tasty mushrooms, and the piece of anthill, with all the shiny black ants swarming over it, in front of the bear. It opened its eyes and lapped up a few of the ants, but soon it seemed to fall asleep again. It was not a well bear. I ate the rest of the ants and half of the mushrooms.

Finally Cossypha came down off the hill, and Rufik scrambled to meet her. Her face was very white. The Prince flung his arms around her and hugged her, and then, embarrassed, he came and bent his red cheeks over the bear. But his ears blushed, too, and Cossypha winked at me, then sighed and looked at the bear.

"How is it?"

I felt its nose.

"It's very hot. I think it has a fever. My nose doesn't feel like that at all."

"It smells like it's sick," observed Banner, strolling over, and Darby followed, looking over her shoulder.

"The horses say the bear smells like it's sick," I told the humans. "I think they're right."

"At least out here there's air," said the bear, waking up.

Air and sun, to shine on my bones,
when they lie white among the stones.

And it sighed.

"Don't say that," I said, and wiped my eyes so that Rufik wouldn't see I was crying. Just a little. "Don't. Cossypha can make you better. You're going to, aren't you, Cossy?"

"I'm going to try," she said quietly. "But you'd better tell it that it might not work."

"It's asleep again," I said.

Cossypha lit two small fires, one on each side of the bear. She put honeysuckle wood and blossoms on them, and the flame was pink. Then she sat down with the bear's head in her lap, and looked sternly at Rufik and me.

"You have to be very, very quiet," she said. "It would be better if you went away altogether. Because I don't know what might happen."

We went a little ways away, but not too far. Rufik was so nervous he held my hand. With the bear's head in her lap, Cossypha started to sing.

The song was in that funny language again. Personally I think Sporryl made it up just for writing spells. It went on and on and on.

"No wonder she was so worried about getting something wrong," whispered Rufik to me. "I could never remember all that if I read it a hundred times."

"Shh," I said.

The bear's fur was all glowing pink, Cossypha was pink too; everything was, in the light of the two little fires. They turned the whole hillside rosy. Then suddenly the bear yipped, like someone had trodden on its toe, and the fires died away to white ash in a breath, and Cossypha fell over on the bear.

Rufik and I ran to her, and the Prince laid her tenderly under a honeysuckle bush, with a cloak under her head.

"She's asleep," he said.

"Magic can be very tiring," I said. "That's why the Enchanter was always so grumpy. Look at the bear."

"Did it turn into a hippopompous?" asked Rufik, not looking away from Cossypha.

"-potamus," I said. "No, but look at it."

Rufik finally looked at it, and frowned.

"Was it that colour when it came out of the hill?"

"No," I said. "But I think it's kind of pretty."

Before, the bear had been black, like most of the bears in the Wild Forest. Now parts of it were still black, and parts were gingery-coloured.

"Like me," said a gingery-coloured bear from the back of the audience somewhere.

"SHHH!" said Bobbin the goblin sternly.

"That bear was probably your grandfather's grandfather's grandfather," the purple toad-thing told the bear. The toad was very old. "I think I met that spotted bear once."

"BE QUIET," said the goblin.

It was in fact a sort of mottled, patchwork bear. Rufik felt its hind leg and said in amazement, "Torrie, feel here! The bone's whole!"

"Of course it is," I said. "That was the point of the spell."

Rufik took the splint off, and the bear woke up with a start.

"I'm hungry," it said, and stretched and stood up. "My, but I feel frisky."

It frisked a bit, and the horses backed away nervously. Then it ate the leftover mushrooms in one gulp, and smacked its lips.

"Thank you, Torrie," it said.

"You should thank the Enchantress," I told it, "when she wakes up. She cured you with magic."

The bear bowed solemnly toward Cossypha, who was still asleep, and frisked some more.

"Come on, Torrie," it said. "Let's go find another ant hill."

"All right," I said. "And we should find a nice reflecting pond. There's something you should see."

When we got back, stuffed with ants, Cossy and Rufik were sitting together on the same rock, eating bread and cheese. The bear capered up to her and bowed again.

"It says, thank you for saving its life, and it quite likes its new colour," I said.

Cossypha blushed and said it was very welcome.

"It's a very handsome colour to be, I think," whispered the gingery bear to the hazel dryad, very quietly, because Torrie was starting to frown.

"We were just wondering," said Rufik, "if the bear knew anything about the Sword."

"What sword?" I asked.

"Wormbane," said Rufik. "The magic, dragon-killing Sword. We are on a Quest, have you forgotten? While we go gallivanting through the forest, Erythroth is being laid waste by a dragon."

"Oh yes," I said, and asked the bear.

"Wormbane?" it asked. "Are you sure it was *Wormbane* you wanted? Some other sword wouldn't do?"

"You know about Wormbane?" I shouted, jumping up and down. "Where is it?"

"Quite near," said the bear. "But are you sure you want it? It's very dangerous, the place where the Sword is supposed to be. No one has actually seen it, of course. But I'm sure there are other Magic Swords around."

"The Hero says it has to be this one," I said.

"Well," said the bear, and thought a bit. "You've saved my life, and if you really want this Sword, I suppose I shall come along and help you get it. But getting it is likely to be very, very dangerous."

"That's all right," I said. "Rufik's a Hero. He likes

danger. Rufik, the bear says it knows where the Sword Wormbane is, and it'll help us get it. But it might be very dangerous, and are you sure another sword won't do?"

"Wormbane!" repeated Rufik, jumping up. "The bear knows where it is? Let's start at once."

"I," said Cossypha, "am going to finish my dinner first."

So we all sat down and the bear and I had another dinner, bread and cheese this time. Ants are very spicy.

After dinner we started along another forest trail, following the bear to where the Sword Wormbane was hidden. The bear sang:

> The Hero, the Lady, and Torrie and me,
> Are all on a Quest together;
> Find a Sword, kill a monster, and save
>   Erythroth,
> An adventure in wonderful weather.

"What do you think?" he asked me proudly.

"Hmmm," said I, thoughtfully. "Someday you should meet Cossypha's father's Court Poet, if he ever gets disenchanted. He might be able to help you more."

Chapter Seven

IN WHICH WE FIND GOBLINS

"*Goblins!*" *said Bobbin. "At last. Now this story is getting good! Do the goblins eat Cossypha? I hope so. I hope they eat the silly Prince too.*"

"*Do you want them to eat the bear, too?*" *asked the gingery bear in a low growl.*

"*I don't care,*" *said Bobbin. "As long as someone gets eaten.*"

The bear pushed through the crowd of nymphs and sat down behind Bobbin.

"*You know,*" *it said, "I've heard of bears eating goblins.*

I'd kind of like to hear if the patchwork bear gets to eat any, while it's helping Rufik and Cossypha find the Sword."

And it yawned, a very wide, pink yawn, and ran its tongue over its sharp, white teeth, so much longer than Bobbin's.

"Go on with the story, Torrie," said the gingery bear. "And let's see what happens to those noisy goblins."

The purple toad-thing giggled.

Bobbin was very, very quiet.

We had travelled for several days back toward the mountains before Rufik even noticed we had changed directions.

"Torrie," he said. "Isn't your bear making a mistake? We're almost back where we started."

"No, this is a different part of the mountains," said Cossypha. "It's around here that goblins live."

"But don't we want to be in the Wild Forest?" asked Rufik.

I asked the bear about it.

"No," said the bear. "Wormbane, the Magic Sword you want, is in the mountains. Some goblins have it. Well, they don't actually have it. It's in a cave, or so I've heard, and the goblins have the cave."

I told Rufik this.

"I don't understand," said the Prince.

"He will," said the bear.

That day we began to climb back into the mountains. We had to leave the horses in a sheltered valley, because the way became too steep and stony for them. Which was really a shame, as fighting goblins was about the only thing Darby was good for.

We walked along a stony path that rapidly became a steep, narrow ledge on the mountainside. The patchwork bear went first, then Cossypha, then Rufik, then me. The ledge grew steeper and steeper, until we were climbing nearly straight up the mountainside, with rocks on the right and nothing but air on the left. Far, far below was the green valley, and in it, a blue black speck and a reddish brown one that were Darby and Banner, grazing in happy green peace, while we got closer and closer to goblins and danger. The patchwork bear was not a very fat bear, because of being starved in the cave for a week, but it rubbed one shaggy side along the rock, and the other was ruffled by the wind from the valley below. It was a good thing both Cossypha and Rufik were skinny.

"I don't want to look down," said Rufik.

"Then don't," said Cossypha. She was used to these sort of mountain trails, although around her father's castle they had been wide enough to ride on or at least wide enough to lead a horse on, carefully.

"I can't help looking, though," said the Prince. "I think I'm going to be sick." He swayed a little. "Are those specks down there the *horses*?"

"You can't be sick," I said. "Think about the Sword. We're almost there. Think about fighting goblins."

"I've never had to fight anything," said Rufik. "I don't think I'm very good at it. I think the goblins will kill me before I ever get back to the Dragon."

"Then your father's kingdom will be destroyed," said Cossypha, "and all the people will be eaten. You're their Hero."

"I know," said Rufik, "but I don't think I'm a very good one. Cossypha, what if I'm not a Hero at all? What will happen then?"

"This is not the place to think about that," I said sternly.

"You have to be a Hero," said Cossypha. "For the sake of your people. Now come on. I've fought goblins before, they're not so bad."

"We are so!" yelped Bobbin, and the ginger bear growled, very softly.

"Go on," I said, and prodded the Prince forward. "Don't think about it. Cossy and I fight goblins for fun, all the time. They're like rats. They were always trying to break into the castle and eat the servants, before

Sporryl turned all the servants into wolf-headed guards, that is. Then they just tried to raid the pantry and steal chickens. But once Cossy and I started following them back to their lairs, they stopped that, too. We're great warriors; all the goblins for miles around the castle fear us."

"Be quiet, Torrie," said Cossypha. "He's exaggerating, Rufik. And besides, we hardly ever came out this way; these goblins won't have heard about us. They'll be eager to fight."

"Tell the humans to be quieter," said the bear to me. "We're getting close."

"Shh, humans," I said.

Cossypha strung her bow and held an arrow ready. Rufik drew his sword.

"Why am I in front?" muttered the patchwork bear to itself, as it crept slowly along the steep path.

"Because I'm smart enough to be at the back," I told it.

Rufik looked at Cossypha, creeping along after the bear, not afraid in the least, and he drew a deep breath.

"I am a Crown Prince and a Knight," he said to himself, but of course I listened. "I am a Hero, and it is my Quest. And she is doing everything heroic so far, she and Torrie. She rescued me, and Torrie got us away from the wolf guards, and they rescued the bear and saved its life. I have to start being heroic sometime, and now would be good, seeing as I've been practicing all my life. I have to be a Hero, to be worthy of my kingdom's faith in me. And to be worthy of her."

With that, he too followed the bear, up the path toward the goblins.

I'd known he was in love with Cossy all along.

The path suddenly broadened into a rocky plateau, like a shelf on the mountain. There was a dark crack in the side of the mountain's rocky wall.

"That," said the bear, "is the entrance to the goblins' cave."

I told Rufik and Cossypha this.

"And do the goblins have the Sword Wormbane?" asked Rufik. "Why would they want a dragon-slaying sword?"

I asked the bear, and repeated his answer to the two humans.

"The goblins don't have the Sword. But a long, long time ago, the Sword and some other treasures were put in the cave by a Sorceress, so that they would be safe until the Hero and his comrades came. The goblins moved in later."

"You mean this Sorceress knew we were coming?" asked Rufik in awe.

"Well, she knew a Hero was coming," I said. "I don't suppose it had to be you."

"Of course it did," said Cossypha. "Otherwise, there

wouldn't be a prophesy about a Hero using Wormbane to save the kingdom of Erythroth, would there?"

"Well," said Rufik, looking brave and heroic, "let's go find out if the Sorceress was right."

"I'll just wait out here," said the bear. I thought about staying with it, to make sure we weren't surprised by an attack from the rear.

"Come on, Torrie," said Cossypha, so I picked up a rock and followed her. The bear followed me, too curious to wait after all.

Goblins, as you probably know, like to sleep during the day. They snore dreadfully.

Torrie paused, but Bobbin didn't say anything.

The entrance to the goblin cave was very narrow, but after about twenty feet Rufik, who was in front, suddenly stumbled out into a chamber like the inside of a huge globe. The tunnel had been blacker than night, but here all the rock was lit with a bluish light. In the middle of the chamber was a high stone table, and on it lay three objects: a sword, a book, and a spear. The blue light came from the table itself, and everywhere; it shone on the wrinkled, hairy, grey hides of goblins. They were sleeping in heaps and tumbles all around the cave, and all around the table. The biggest, ugliest goblin was right at Rufik's feet.

"Go on," I whispered. "Go take the Sword."

"But it's a Magic Sword," Rufik whispered back. "It's been hidden here for centuries, surely I can't just stroll over and wander off with it. Shouldn't there be some kind of test, or a mysterious Lady to proclaim me worthy of it, or something?"

"You've listened to too many tales," Cossypha hissed. "It's here, and you're here, and that's all the magic it needs. If you aren't the right Hero, you won't be able to take it, so stop being silly and go get it, before the goblins wake up."

"Right," said Rufik, forgetting to whisper, and he stepped over the sleeping goblin toward the table on which the Sword lay. The goblin woke up.

"Thieves!" it shrieked, and reached for Rufik's ankles with long-clawed fingers. I dropped my rock on its head. Goblins have very thick skulls; it howled and scrambled away unharmed. All the other goblins woke up and began howling and yelling and leaping around.

"Look out!" shrieked Cossypha as two goblins leapt off a ledge on the wall. One fell to the floor with her arrow through its throat; the other landed on Rufik, clawing and biting. Cossy dropped her bow and drew her sword.

"Let's go, Goblins!" cheered Bobbin, and ran up a tree before the gingery bear could even open its mouth.

73

Rufik knocked the goblin off his head, so he could see to use his sword again, and the two humans fought back to back, in the middle of a ring of ugly grey goblins who beat at them with sticks and stones and claws. The patchwork bear reared up on its hind legs, growling, and some of the goblins shrieked and fled down the tunnel into the sunlight they hated. The bear knocked a few more outside, tossing them like pine cones. I looked around and could find nothing at all to fight with, so I picked up my rock and threw it again. Then one of the goblins picked me up and threw *me*! I sailed through the air.

"And I bet you screamed all the way!" called Bobbin from up in the tree.

I sailed through the air, *Torrie began again, a little louder,* and landed on the stone table in the middle of the blue light. There was the Sword Wormbane, with strange letters etched on its blade, there was a thick, leather-bound book, dark with age, and there was a spear, a very short spear for a human, only tall enough to be a walking stick, with a beautiful bronze point on it, no iron at all. All you animals know that we Old Creatures hate the touch of iron.

Well, there I was on the table, and there was the bear, bowling goblins out the door, and there were Cossypha and the Prince, surrounded by goblins and dead goblins. And there was the biggest goblin of all, the one I had first dropped a stone on, with a huge stone axe, creeping up beside the humans, who were too busy to notice it in the press of goblins. I didn't dare touch Wormbane, not only was it magic and meant for Rufik, but it was iron besides. I grabbed the bronze-headed spear and threw it with all my strength, and that was the end of that goblin.

"Look!" shrieked a goblin. "It's taken one of the table-things!"

And all the goblins started screaming and yelling worse than ever, and they all tried to flee out the tunnel. They nearly got stuck, so many of them tried to squeeze through at once, but the bear hurried them on their way.

Suddenly we four were alone in the cave.

CHAPTER EIGHT

IN WHICH WE MEET THE WOLF GUARDS AGAIN

"*All the goblins went to lie in wait and ambush you when you came out,*" *said Bobbin up in the tree.* "*Just wait and see, you'll all get killed when you try to leave the cave.*"

"*Obviously we won't,*" *said Torrie,* "*because we didn't. I'm still here.*" *And he stuck out his tongue at Bobbin.*

"*What happened next, Torrie?*" *asked the purple toad-thing.*

"I've never seen so many goblins," said Cossypha,

and sat down on the floor. The bear sat down beside her and she put her arm around its neck. Rufik was standing at the table.

"Look, Cossypha," he said softly. "It's the Sword. It's Wormbane. We've found it."

Cossypha just nodded.

"I've found something, too," I said. "It was on the table."

I held up the spear. It was just the right height for me. (It still is, too, and if a certain goblin doesn't keep quiet, I'll start using it on goblins again.)

Cossypha looked at the spear, and at the table, and suddenly stood up again.

"There's a spell on the table," she said, "and it's starting to come undone. I think we should take the Sword and leave quickly."

"There's a book, too," said Rufik, never looking away from the table. "I think you should have it, Cossypha. I can't read what's written on the cover, but it looks sorcerous."

He picked up the book, very carefully, and handed it to Cossypha. She tucked it under one arm, and picked up her bow again with the other.

"Let's leave," she said nervously. Rufik didn't hear her. Slowly, he grasped the hilt of the Sword Wormbane. The blue light disappeared. We were in complete and utter darkness. The mountain rumbled to itself.

"We have to leave *now*," said Cossypha, and suddenly there was a faint ball of light hovering in front of the tunnel. "Follow the light, everyone, and let's get out of here."

We had barely stumbled out into the sunlight when there came a creaking, groaning crash, and a cloud of dust billowed out after us.

"Just like *my* cave," said the patchwork bear.

"This cave was just for the Sword," said Cossypha, coughing. "Once it was taken, the cave's purpose was over. The goblins knew that, that's why they ran away when they saw Torrie could take the spear. Come on, let's go get the horses."

There wasn't a goblin in sight as we hiked back down to the valley; they had all crawled into other dark caves and crevices. Rufik walked dreamily along, holding the Sword Wormbane before him, never noticing how steep and narrow the path was, or how far down he could fall. He only looked around him when we were in the valley again.

"Now," he said, "I must return to Erythroth, to fight the Dragon. I will come back to you if I can."

"But we're coming with you," said Cossypha.

"We didn't rescue you so you could go off and get eaten by a dragon alone," I said.

"But it will be dangerous," said the Prince. "More dangerous than you can imagine. I can't take my friends into that kind of peril."

"You're not taking us," said Cossypha. "We're coming."

The day before Rufik would have tried to argue with us. Today, covered in scratches and bruises and goblinbites, he was older, wiser—a Hero. And he knew when he was beaten.

"Very well," he said, and smiled. "I'd be very lonely if you didn't come."

He was looking at Cossypha when he said this.

"You'd be lonely without me, too," I said.

We made a fire in the valley and had a feast; at least, we called it a feast. The patchwork bear and I found raspberry canes growing among the rocks on the mountainside, so we had raspberries and cheese and old dry bread, which was all we had to eat now anyhow. We toasted the cheese on sticks over the fire and drank tea and sang silly songs, and Rufik sat with his arm around Cossypha's shoulders.

"Isn't it lovely?" said Rufik's horse, Banner. "To be young, and in love."

"Well, you're certainly not young," said Darby, which wasn't true, and Banner snorted and kicked at him, just playing, and he tossed his horns and chased her around the valley.

"What's in the book, Cossy?" I asked, and for the first time Cossypha remembered the book from the cave, and opened it on her lap. Rufik looked over her shoulder, and I climbed up on his shoulder to look over both. The bear decided to have a nap.

The pages were all creamy yellow, the strange writing was all in purple ink, and around the margins were tiny pictures in colours still bright. Red and green and blue and yellow, even gold in places. Tiny humans and animals and plants wound around them.

"It's a book of spells," said Cossypha, reading slowly to herself. We watched her finger tracing along the lines of letters. "The language isn't quite like Father's, but I can figure it out. This first page is, well, it's a letter. 'You who take this book from the cave, you who will join the Hero against the Dragon, this is yours, to aid you in your life…'. There's a great deal more. It's rather, well, it's odd. She knew everything. About running away because Father had become an evil magician. She says…" Cossypha was silent, still reading.

"What does she say?" I asked.

"Torrie," said Rufik. "It might be personal."

"So?" I said. "I'm her bestest friend; it's not too personal for me."

"We have to go back to Erythroth by way of Father's castle," said Cossypha suddenly.

"Why?" asked Rufik.

"Because we do," said Cossypha.

"It might be difficult," said Rufik, "because of the wolf guards."

"We'll manage," said Cossypha.

So it was decided that we should ride along a trail Cossypha and I knew of that wound through the mountains to Sporryl's castle. The patchwork bear was going to return to the Wild Forest. It did not feel properly at home in the mountains, it said, and would not be much use at dragon-hunting. It recited one last poem before we parted.

> Across the tall mountains and into the woods,
> And back to the mountains they came.
> They found a great sword and a book and a spear,
> Fought some goblins and won lasting fame.
> They conquered the goblins and set out again,
> To seek for a dragon or two,
> And when they have found it, the Heroes so bold,
> I've no doubt they will conquer it too.

The bear was very proud of its latest poem, which I repeated for the humans. Cossypha kissed it on the nose and called it a dear bear, and Rufik shook its paw. Then it said goodbye to the horses and me, and trotted down out of the valley, singing its little song to itself as it went.

"I hope the dragon isn't 'or two'," said Rufik. "I'm not feeling *that* heroic."

The next day we travelled along a winding mountain trail that joined up with one we knew well. Rufik rode in front, with me to tell him the way, because sometimes it seemed as if the path had vanished completely, if you didn't know it was there. The horses went slowly, taking care with each step. Sometimes loose rocks would rattle away underfoot. Every now and then Rufik or I would look back at Cossypha. She rode even more slowly than we did, letting Darby pick his own way, which was fine, as he knew the trail almost as well as I did. The reins lay loose on his neck, and Cossypha read her book. She never looked up, not even when a rock kicked up by Banner bounced away down the mountainside, starting a rumbling rock slide below us.

Long after Rufik was asleep that night she read in the light of our campfire, and I stayed up to keep it going for her. She ate her breakfast without seeing it, and read as we rode the final miles back to her father's castle. Just as it loomed into sight, a dark grey, spiky building leaning over the narrow mountain pass, she closed the book with a sigh and looked around, rubbing her eyes.

"Finished," she said.

"I think we're in trouble again," said Rufik, and pointed. There were wolf guards riding up toward us, looking nasty. Of course, they always looked nasty. Behind us, real wolves started to howl.

"This story's getting good at last," said Bobbin. "Torrie's going to get eaten."

Chapter Nine

IN WHICH SPORRYL WANTS HIS DAUGHTER BACK

"You two look after the wolves," Cossypha ordered, and rode slowly down to meet the wolf guards. They had drawn their swords, but looked as if they weren't quite certain what to do next.

"Right," said Rufik, and wheeled Banner around to face up the trail. I jumped down onto a rock and waved my bronze-headed spear at the wolves.

"I took this spear from an enchanted, goblin-infested cave," I called to them. "It was put there for me hundreds of years ago by a great Sorceress. Run away now if you don't want to know any more about it!"

The wolves howled and laughed at me.

"I wonder if it would be polite to use Wormbane to fight a pack of flea-bitten wolves?" Rufik asked himself. "It doesn't seem quite right to me."

He had carried the Magic Sword strapped to the saddle under his knee. Now he patted it, saying, "Your turn will come," and drew his old sword.

Behind us, one of the wolf guards was saying sternly, "Your father wants to talk to you, Milady."

"He hasn't wanted to talk to me since my mother died," said Cossypha, "and that was before I can remember, as you know very well. I have come back, with my friends, to help you and to help Lord Sporryl, my father. He is going to have to give up being an evil Enchanter."

The wolf guards laughed.

"You can tell him so yourself, Your Ladyship."

I turned around. Sure enough, Lord Sporryl in his dusty purple robes was riding up behind the wolf guards.

"Cossypha!" he said, once he had come up to where she sat on Darby. "Go back to the castle at once. I will speak to you later. How dare you allow this foolish prince to steal you?"

"I stole him," said Cossypha. "I didn't think you would notice if I was here or not. There was no good reason for me to stay here, when you never talked to me from one day to the next. Why don't you give up being evil and go back to being a normal Magician? You must have been once."

"Don't you talk to me that way, young lady," said Sporryl. "Go to your room at once."

Cossypha laughed at him. The Enchanter stared as if he couldn't believe it, and his face got redder and redder.

"I'm not a child any more, Father. You are going to give up being evil whether you want to or not. I've come back to help you, even though you don't want me to."

Sporryl sputtered. "I'm going to turn your prince into a toad!" he finally managed to roar.

"You can try," said Cossypha politely.

Sporryl drew a deep breath and began a spell. Cossypha looked at him sadly, and read three words from the last page of her spell book. There was a great cloud of purple smoke; it filled the entire cut in the mountains where the castle stood, and standing on my rock I could not even see Banner's leg beside me. I poked her to make sure she was still there, and she stamped and snorted, so I knew everybody hadn't disappeared. The wolves were whimpering in fear.

"Flee for you lives!" I shouted to them, in wolf-speech of course. "Or the mighty Enchantress Cossypha will turn you all into little brown mice!"

The wolves started yelping, and I could hear their

claws scrabbling on the rocks. Then there was no sound at all in the purple smoke, except for somebody coughing softly.

Slowly, the wind blew the smoke away.

I turned around. The first thing I saw was Darby.

"Darby!" I shrieked, and started to laugh. I had to sit down on my rock. The wolves were all gone, so Rufik turned around too. He started to laugh as well, and so did Banner. Darby swung his head around and glared at us, then he realized something was wrong, and his ears went back. He had no horns. He shook his head. No horns. He rubbed his nose on his knee. It was the wrong colour. I laughed and laughed. Darby was a very ordinary, brown horse. So were the horses of all the wolf guards, and of Sporryl himself. They weren't all brown, of course. Some were bay, and white, and grey, and black, and spotted. But none of them were beetle-coloured, and not one had horns.

The wolf guards were looking at their horses, and then, in amazement, at one another. No wolf-heads! One of them howled for joy, and started to laugh, because he sounded like man imitating a wolf very badly, and the rest started laughing at him, and running their hands through their hair and beards—except the women had no beards—and feeling their noses to make sure they were real. The captain of the wolf guards spurred his grey horse forward and swept Cossypha out of the saddle and hugged her. It was the Court Poet.

"You've done it!" he shouted, laughing and crying at once. "Little Cossy, you've done it! We're free! Three cheers for Cossypha, men!" The men (and women) cheered.

"Ahem," said Rufik, riding up, and the Court Poet put Cossypha down and shook Rufik's hand. "Delighted to meet you again, Your Highness," he said.

I climbed up on Darby. "Brown," he muttered to me. "Plain, dull brown."

"You look very nice," I told him, only half-listening. I was looking at Sporryl.

The Enchanter, now riding a piebald horse, black-and-white spotted, was looking around him in horror.

"What have you done?" he wailed.

"I've undone all your spells," said Cossypha quietly. "And you'll find, Father, that you won't be able to cast any more. I've taken away all your magic. You were doing too much harm, and no good, with it. That's not what magic is for."

"Horrible child!" cried the powerless Enchanter, and pulled his horse around to gallop back to the castle.

"Father!" Cossypha shouted after him. "Come visit me in Erythroth!" And she burst into tears.

"He didn't mean it," I said, and pulled her hair to make her listen. "Cossy, he didn't really mean it."

"I know," she sobbed into my fur. "But it doesn't make any difference."

"She should have turned him into a toad," said Bobbin. "I would have."

Rufik came and put his arms around her too, and so did the Court Poet. It was still me she held onto though, even if she was going to marry the Prince. The Court Poet gave her a handkerchief. Rufik looked at my dripping fur and gave me one.

"Sporryl will get over it," said the Court Poet. "He hasn't been quiet right in his mind since your mother died, you know. Perhaps the shock of losing his magic will make him see sense. He used to be a good man, until he decided not to care for anybody. He even hated himself, you know."

"I know," said Cossypha, and sniffed. "Will you and the others stay here and look after him? We have to go to Erythroth and kill a dragon."

"Of course," said the Court Poet.

"You could try and make him come to Erythroth," said Cossypha, and blew her nose. "If he decides to become good again. Don't tell him, Poet, but the spell didn't really take his magic powers away. Not forever. They'll come back in a month, but it might be better if he doesn't realize that. Not until he's had time to think about everything."

"Right," said the Court Poet. "And I'll certainly try to get him to Erythroth for you. Is there anything else I can do, to help you on your way?"

"Food," I said. The Court Poet could neither see nor hear me.

"Food," said Rufik. "I'm afraid our supplies are running out."

"I'll send one of the men back to bring you food," said the Poet. "It might be best if you didn't come up to the castle."

It was the Poet himself who rode out with packs of food. More cheese, smoked sausages and dried meat, the last of last fall's apples, onions, and a kind of bread humans call hardtack, which will keep forever and is good for sharpening your teeth on. Horrible stuff to eat, though.

"Don't you worry, Lady Cossypha," said the Poet as we prepared to ride back to Erythroth on the other side of the mountains. "Your father will soon be himself again. I'll see to it."

So we rode back out along the mountain pass, where Rufik had first been captured by the wolf guards. Behind us, the Court Poet stood on a rock and waved.

"Good luck with the Dragon!" he called.

"I don't know about this story," said Bobbin. "First the bear doesn't eat you, then the goblins don't eat you, now the wolves don't eat you. What kind of story is this, where nobody gets eaten? And why didn't the Enchantress turn

her father into a toad? Treating her like that! She should have turned him into a toad, and then Torrie could have eaten him."

"Toads aren't good to eat," said the purple toad-thing.

"I don't know," said Bobbin, and smacked her lips. "Once in a while.... Are there any more nuts down there? Or maybe some mushrooms?"

"No!" said almost everybody.

"Oh well," said Bobbin, and ate a few leaves. "Maybe the Dragon will get to eat somebody."

"I'm going to climb that tree in a minute," said the gingery bear. "And then somebody will get eaten, for sure."

"This story's going to end right here, if you guys can't be quiet," said Torrie. "Then you'll never find out what happens, ever. And serves you right."

Chapter Ten

IN WHICH WE FIND THE DRAGON

"Is everybody going to be quiet?" asked Torrie.

"Yes," said the gingery bear.

"Do you promise?"

"Maybe," said the goblin. "Get on with the story. I want to know about the Dragon."

The land of Erythroth was very green and fair. Not at all what I expected of a kingdom to which a dragon had been laying waste. I said so to the Prince.

"The Dragon hasn't come this far yet," said Rufik.

"Oh," I said. "Maybe it won't. Maybe it'll stay where it is. Or go away."

Rufik just laughed.

"There aren't any people," said Cossypha. "I haven't seen any since we came out of the mountains."

"Everyone has fled to the coast," explained the Prince. "That's where my father's capital city is. They hope the royal knights and the army can protect that one city at least, if the Dragon gets that far. Or they can flee in ships to some other kingdom, if all is lost."

I thought about what that would mean. If all was lost, we would not have killed the Dragon; it would have eaten us.

"Except they won't have to flee," I said," because you're going to slay it."

"I hope so," said Rufik glumly.

"Don't talk like that," said Cossypha. "You have the Magic Sword, Wormbane. And me, and Torrie."

"Especially us," I said. "The Dragon doesn't stand a chance. It's not a very large dragon, is it?"

"It's supposed to be enormous," Rufik said.

"I knew it," said Bobbin, from up in her tree. "You're going to get eaten by the Dragon."

"I did not get eaten by a dragon!" shouted Torrie, and whacked a charred branch with his spear, so that the sparks snapped and flew.

"Go on with the story," said the deer-footed imp.

I looked at my new spear, tied to the bundles behind Darby's saddle. It must be ancient; it had been in that cave with the sword and the book of magic for hundreds of years. Waiting, just for me. Just so I could help Rufik in his battle against the Dragon. Knowing that should have made me feel bold and heroic, but it didn't. I was scared. Just a little. After all, dragons are an awful lot bigger than me. A dragon could probably use the spear for a toothpick.

Cossypha wasn't afraid at all, of course. She was never scared of anything.

"Torrie," she whispered to me as we rode.

"What?"

"Are you afraid?"

"Not at all," I said bravely.

"Oh," said Cossypha.

After a while she said, "Torrie?"

"What?"

"I am."

"Oh," I said, and thought about that. "It doesn't matter," I said finally, and climbed up so I could whisper in her ear. "I'm scared too."

Cossypha laughed. She hadn't laughed much at all since we had left the mountains and her magic-less father.

"What's so funny?" asked Rufik over his shoulder.

"Nothing," I said. "It's a personal joke. What happens if we can't find the Dragon?"

"That shouldn't be a problem," said the Prince, becoming glum again. "It will likely find us."

Nevertheless, we travelled for almost a week through the green countryside without seeing any sign of the Dragon. Except that all the people had fled to the seacoast. No farmers were in the fields, although the grain was beginning to show golden instead of green. No smoke rose from the chimneys of the houses. When we rode through the empty villages, there were not even any dogs to come barking at our heels. All the people, all the animals, were gone. Which was really too bad. I had been looking forward to warm, foamy milk or a nice roast fowl, here in this green land.

But the villagers had taken even the oldest and scrawniest of hens with them. Perhaps they hoped that if there was nothing for the Dragon to eat when it came that way, it would turn and go back to wherever it had come from, and not ravage any further into Erythroth. So we ate the food that the Court Poet, who had once been the captain of the wolf guards, had packed for us, and once in a while Rufik went fishing.

Then one day we suddenly came upon the Dragon. It was morning, a beautiful, sunny, peaceful-seeming morning, with dew glittering on spider webs in the grass. Rufik was carefully burying the ashes of our fire when Cossypha said, "Look," in such a grim tone that even the horses stopped grazing and looked. She pointed to the far horizon.

"Smoke," said Rufik, and for a moment my breakfast felt like an eel swimming in my belly.

"Maybe it's just a grass fire," I said, so quietly that the humans didn't hear.

Banner nickered and stamped a hoof.

"I knew it. I dreamed about dragons all last night."

"I wish we were back in the mountains," said Darby, lowering his head to rub his horns on a rock, before remembering that he didn't have horns any more.

"Cheer up, Brownie," said Banner, winking at me.

"Brownie?" neighed Darby. "Brownie! You...you..." He spluttered and snorted, and lunged at Banner, trying to bite her neck. She wheeled away, showing her heels, and the humans ran up shouting, "Whoa there," and "Hey!"

"What's gotten into the horses, Torrie?" asked the Prince.

"They're excited about the Dragon," I lied cheerfully.

"Brownie," muttered Darby to himself. "Brownie! I'll show her."

"Shhh," I said. "You are brown now, and I've known some very nice brownies in my time."

"I don't care," said Darby. "I used to be black like a

beetle, and very handsome. It's not fair."

"Silly," I said. "We've got more important things to worry about than what colour you are. Beetle colour was just one of Sporryl's enchantments. You've always really been brown."

"I was just trying to take his mind off the Dragon," said Banner helpfully. "I had no idea he'd be so upset. I think Darby's really much better looking now than he was when he had horns."

"Really?" asked Darby.

"Really."

"And," I said, "it's a very nice brown. Like…like well-polished walnut wood."

"Oh," said Darby, and swished his tail happily.

I sighed. "Cossy, you have a very vain horse."

Before we rode off that morning Rufik put on his armour. He had a long chain mail shirt that came to his knees, with a gold and red surcoat over it, a round shield with a gold dog on a red background, and a helmet that had a gold dog on its crest. That was the Royal Hound of Erythroth, he told us. He looked very handsome and heroic. Cossypha told him so and he blushed. With the Sword Wormbane slung at his side he seemed almost invincible. If only the Dragon would think so, too.

I sat behind Cossypha, looking back over Darby's tail the way we had come. It was very beautiful, very green.

I didn't like to think of it all black and smoking, but I didn't like to think of me all black and smoking either. Rufik jingled whenever he moved, but armour would not keep the Dragon from burning him to a cinder. And Cossypha was only wearing her goblin-hunting leather jerkin and leggings. I couldn't let Cossypha get burned.

"We need a plan," I said out loud.

I expected Rufik to say something like, "I thought we would just ride up and challenge the Dragon, isn't that a plan?" but he didn't. Instead he frowned.

"You're right," he said. "I've been trying to think of one. In all the books I've read, the knight just rides up to it and they fight, but it seems to me that if the Dragon sees me coming, it's going to breathe fire and I'll never get close to it. We have to catch it unawares. Do dragons sleep?"

"They must sometime," said Cossypha.

"In the night or in the day?" asked Rufik practically.

Cossy shook her head. "I have no idea. There was only a little about them in the *Book of Beasts* in Father's library, and even less in the *Natural History*. The *Natural History* said they had a soft spot under the jaw, though," she added more hopefully. "That's something."

We kept riding on toward the Dragon while the humans talked about all the battles with dragons they had read of in books. I didn't see how that would help, but

I didn't say anything. I climbed up so I could look over Cossypha's shoulder. The black smoke on the horizon was very close now. It got closer and closer. I still couldn't think of any useful plan at all. The horses walked slower and slower, and neither the Prince nor Cossypha said anything at all now.

The smoke seemed to drift lazily up over the next long, high hill. On this side of the hill were a few birches and maple trees and here and there a lacy hackmatack. It was just a little woods, with a trickle of water winding down in a deep, ferny ditch to join a calm, brown brook at the bottom. With one accord the horses stopped, reluctant to enter this, the last valley before the Dragon.

A cow path meandered down our hill, across the brook, over the trickle from the spring where it ran out of the woods, and up along the edge of the trees until it disappeared over the top of the next hill. There was a single tall tree there, a black, stiff skeleton of a tree. The smoke curled around its topmost branches, and even the humans could smell it over the sweet scent of the white clover around the horses' feet. For a long time no one said anything.

"Why don't I go scout on ahead?" I heard myself say.

No one said, "Oh no, Torrie, it would be too dangerous." Instead, Cossypha nodded. "It might be the best idea. You can sneak through the trees better than anyone. But be careful, Torrie."

"Don't go over the hill," said the Prince. "Just to the top and look over."

"What was on the other side?" asked Bobbin, and climbed down to a lower branch, so that she could hear better.

"Why should you care?" asked the purple toad-thing. "You've been interrupting and being rude all along."

"I want to know," said Bobbin. "Be quiet." And she threw a pine cone at the purple toad-thing.

The gingery bear growled, very softly.

"I haven't got to the top of the hill yet," said Torrie crossly. "Give me time to get there."

He went on:

I got down off of Darby.

"Oh Torrie," said Cossypha suddenly, and she got down and hugged me. "Are you sure you should?"

"Somebody has to," I said. "And I can do it best."

"Take care," said the Prince solemnly, and he dismounted and shook my hand.

"If it's asleep," Banner said, "don't wake it up."

"Scare it away if you can," said Darby. Banner and I both looked at him. "Well," he said, "Torrie's rather scary, if you don't expect him."

"Torrie's rather small," said Banner. "Especially if you're a dragon."

Enough was enough.

Rufik

"Goodbye," I said, and walked bravely down the hill, using my spear as a staff, and waded bravely across the brook, and crept bravely into the trees. There were no birds in the woods, no rabbits or foxes or mice or anything. It was very, very quiet. I walked under the green roof of the bracken more quietly than a fog and wiggled the last little way on my belly into a rhododendron bush. I was at the edge of the woods on the top of the hill. Very, very carefully, I peeked out of the bush.

Chapter Eleven

IN WHICH WE FIGHT THE DRAGON

Everything was black and grey and dead. There was no grass, just grey, ashy earth and rocks and sad black tree stumps. And the Dragon.

It was as big as Sporryl's castle, or would have been if it was curled up in a ball. Stretched out, it was long and snaky and went on forever, around and around in long lazy loops. It was an odd glittery colour, bronze where the sun shone on it, dull green in the shadows. It had great wings like a bat's, spread just a little at its sides to enjoy the sun, and a long, narrow head with big feathery fringes like the fancy plumage of some birds. The tip of its snout was tucked under the tip of its tail, and its eyes were closed. Dragons obviously slept during the day. Or maybe it was having an afternoon nap. It sighed in its sleep, and two wisps of black smoke curled up into the air. And did I mention how very *big* it was?

"Yes," said the deer-footed imp.

"You weren't supposed to answer," said the hazel dryad. "It was a rhetorical question."

"What's a rhetorical question?" asked the deer-footed imp.

"One that you're not supposed to answer," said the dryad.

"But why did he ask a question if he didn't want an answer?" the imp wanted to know. "That's silly."

"Quiet down there," Bobbin ordered.

I lay there in that bush and looked at the Dragon. I couldn't do anything else. I couldn't think; I don't remember if I was even breathing. I was just staring at the Dragon. Finally I remembered what I was doing and began to creep away, backward out of the bush. If I didn't get back soon, Cossy would come looking for me, and the Dragon might hear her rustling through the bracken. Back down through the woods, I stopped where the spring bubbled out of the ground into a pit of green moss and stuck my head in and drank. The water was cold as the rocks deep under the earth, and I felt more awake. Dragons can have a stupefying effect on you if you look at them for too long.

Cossypha had come down off the hilltop and was pacing along the bank of the brook, waiting for me. Rufik was still at the top of our hill, keeping watch in case the Dragon woke up. He would see it there sooner than Cossy would down in the valley. Cossypha didn't say anything, just sighed with relief as I waded back across the brook. We went back up to Rufik.

"Well?" he asked.

"There's definitely a dragon over there," I said.

"Torrie," said the Prince. "Please."

"It's very big," I said.

Rufik didn't say anything.

"It's having a nap," I said, being serious for once. "It's just below the edge of the woods on the top of the hill, or parts of it are. It's really awfully big. I don't know how soundly dragons sleep. We might be able to sneak up on it."

"We'd better take our chance while it's sleeping," said Cossypha. "We'll never get near it otherwise."

"Don't you know any dragon spells?" I asked, just in case.

"No. I don't think there are any," Cossypha said. "There weren't even any in the Book of Spells from the cave." She began stringing her bow. "Their hide is too tough for arrows to do more than annoy them, or so I've read, but I might be able to do something anyway."

"We still absolutely have to get close to it, to use Wormbane," said Rufik, and swung up on Banner's back.

"Right," said Cossypha, and mounted. Rufik leaned over and kissed her. I missed my chance to say something and make her blush, I was too busy thinking.

"Before you go charging over the hill," I said, "let me go on ahead. I'll get around the other side of the Dragon, and we'll have it surrounded. Then I can distract it if it wakes up too soon."

"All right," said Rufik, very solemn.

"I want to go home," said Darby.

I went back down the hill, across the brook, and into the woods again. I looked back just once. Cossypha waved. I went on, wondering why the Dragon couldn't hear my heart beating.

I stuck my head out of the rhododendron bush again, took a deep breath, and crawled out onto the ashy ground. Little swirls of ashes whirled up around me no matter how slowly I moved; I was soon grey from nose to heel. Only my spear still glinted in the light, but the Dragon slept on. Along the side of the beast I crept. Ashes blew up my nose and into my eyes and mouth. My eyes watered and I wanted to sneeze and cough. The

Dragon smelt like burning coal.

Finally I got behind a big charred stump and crouched there, spear ready. What were the humans doing? It seemed forever that I sat there, trying not to sneeze. I couldn't hear the horses coming.

But the Dragon did. Suddenly its head went up, red eyes open. It sniffed the air, tasted it with its tongue, and blew a small snort of fire. I felt like I had a dozen eels writhing in my belly now. I knew, I just knew, that we were all going to die.

The Dragon unfurled its wings and spread them. Ash blew up in a whirlwind. I coughed, but the sound was drowned out in the thunder of hooves from below the crest of the hill. Rufik and Cossypha charged around the corner of the woods.

"For Erythroth!" Rufik shouted.

The Dragon was leaping into the air, ready to scorch them from above.

I howled and sprang over the stump, plunging my spear into the Dragon's foot, which was all I could reach of it. The bronze point pierced the thick scales easily. It was magic, like Wormbane.

"Yarrr!" I howled, and stabbed it in the foot again. And again. Steaming blood bubbled, but the monster was so big! My little spear didn't hurt it any more than a thorn would me. But still, it worked. The Dragon forgot about flying for a moment; its long neck lashed around to see what had bitten it.

"Yarrr!" I howled again, and ran back to stab at its tail. The Dragon snorted. Fire rolled along its side, running off it like water, but the fur on the left side of my body turned to ashes in an instant. I really howled then, I can tell you.

"Torrie!" shouted Cossypha, and the Dragon's head whipped back to Cossy and Rufik.

Cossypha sent an arrow whistling through the air. The Dragon let out a roar of flame and the arrow turned to ash in the air. But the humans' charge never faltered. A second arrow followed the first, sinking deep into the muscle at the base of the Dragon's wing. The monster would have to do its fighting on the ground, now.

"Well done!" cheered Rufik.

Cossypha released a third arrow, but the magic on it failed this time. It rattled harmlessly off the Dragon's scales.

The Dragon spread its wings and tried again to jump into the air. When it realized it couldn't it shrieked horribly and plunged to meet the humans, spewing fire. Cossy threw away her bow and drew her sword, sent Darby twisting away from the fire, galloping along the Dragon's side. Rufik and Banner spun to the other side. The Dragon lashed back and forth between them.

Rufik hacked at the base of its neck. Wormbane shimmered and sang; the Dragon dripped boiling blood but it seemed no weaker.

THE
DRAGON

I was dizzy. My side hurt. My head hurt. I felt like a half-cooked dinner. I could only hold my spear with one hand. I stabbed once more and the Dragon roared and lashed its tail. I went sailing through the air, just like in the goblins' cave, and landed about seven feet off the ground in a burnt tree. I hurt too much to move, so I just hung there with my head spinning.

Rufik struck again at the Dragon's neck and the hot blood spurted. That's it, I thought, that must have killed it, but no, it snapped its head around, seized the Prince in its jaws and dragged him from the saddle.

"Rufik, no!" Cossypha yelled. She attacked the Dragon more furiously than ever. Her plain magic-less sword had been having little effect on it. Now she stood in the stirrups and swung two-handed, with all her might behind the blow. Her sword shattered on the iron-hard scales.

"Look out, Cossy!" I called weakly, but I don't think she heard. Darby did. He wheeled away barely in time as the tail lashed at them.

Cossypha was shouting something, I think it was a spell; there was a sudden burst of smoke and white light in front of the Dragon's face. The beast dropped Rufik and reared up over Cossy. Another swing of its tail bowled Darby over, and while Cossy and Darby tumbled on the ground it spat fire at them again. The Dragon was half-blinded by Cossy's explosion, so most of the flame missed them. They'd have been dead then and there if it hadn't.

Rufik thought they were dead; he screamed "No!" and flung himself toward Cossy. The Dragon grinned and reached down with gaping jaw and gleaming teeth to snatch Rufik from where he stood over Cossypha, and as its head lowered the Prince thrust Wormbane into the soft spot under the jaw that Cossy had read about in the *Natural History*.

The Dragon gurgled and tossed its head up again, flinging Rufik to the ground and spraying everything with blood. It fell over, thrashing and twitching, coughing fire.

Rufik ran to Cossypha and dragged her away before it could roll on her. Its tail knocked Darby flying again. There wasn't anything we could do. We just stayed there, me in the tree and Rufik holding Cossypha, watching. The Dragon twisted and writhed in the ashes with Wormbane still in its throat. Finally there was one last scrabbling twitch and a great roaring cough of smoke, and the Dragon lay motionless.

Rufik helped Cossypha up. Banner nosed at Darby until he rolled over and lifted his head.

"We did it," said Rufik, and kissed Cossypha again. "Cossy, we did it. The Dragon's dead."

"You're not dead, Brownie," said Banner. "Don't go scaring people like that. Get up on your feet."

Darby stood up, as shaky as a foal.

Cossypha kissed Rufik.

I fainted and fell out of the tree.

"Is that the end?" asked Bobbin.

"Don't interrupt," the purple toad-thing said. "How can it be the end? It doesn't sound finished."

"And they have to get married now," said the deer-footed imp.

"That's not important," said Bobbin. "What's important is that they found the Sword and slew the Dragon and Torrie fell out of a tree. I think Torrie falling out of a tree is a very good way to end a story."

"Ahem," said Torrie. "Do you mind?

When I woke up the sun was setting. I was lying on the soft grass beside the brook, and all my burns were wrapped up in some sort of poultice of mushed-up leaves and bark and tied with linen bandages. Cossy was asleep too, with her head in Rufik's lap. They were both bandaged as well, but at least we were all alive. The horses were grazing peacefully side by side, with a few scorched patches themselves. There was no hair on Darby's tail; it looked a bit like a rat's.

"Thank goodness you're awake," said the Prince. "I was getting worried about you."

"I'm fine," I said, and sat up, whimpering a little. I felt like a mangy gobl— rat, I was missing so much fur. "Is Cossy hurt?"

"Burnt," said Rufik. "She's just tired. She had to find the plants for the burn-salve, and then there was some magic involved in making it. I told her I'd stay awake and watch you."

"I wasn't going to go anywhere," I said, and we grinned at one another. "You can go to sleep now, if you like."

Rufik yawned, and carefully lay down and went to sleep, with Cossy using his chest for a pillow now. I snuggled up beside her. She smelt like burnt hair.

We stayed in the valley for two days, resting and eating and not doing much else. Birds had come back already, and when I went to peek over the hill where the Dragon lay, I saw little sprigs of green starting to push up through the ashes. But the Dragon, even dead, was cold and ugly and evil looking, and I went away quickly after I found my spear, which I'd dropped when the Dragon threw me into the tree. Our burns healed quickly, thanks to Cossypha's magic salve, a recipe out of the book from the cave.

The horses and I even started to grow our hair back, but nothing but time, lots of time, would bring back Cossy's hair. I giggled whenever I looked at her.

You remember how I told you Cossypha's copper-coloured hair hung down to her heels, and she wore it braided up on her head most of the time?

"Of course," said the gingery bear. "Some of us have

been paying attention.

"Wasn't that another rhetorical question?" asked the imp.

"Shhh!" said Bobbin.

Well, that had all burned off when she and Darby were knocked down. Now her hair was short, it didn't even come to her shoulders, and after Rufik trimmed the black ends off with his nail scissors, it stuck out around her head like a dandelion.

"I don't look like a dandelion," Cossy said indignantly. "Not at all."

"Well, actually, you do," said Rufik. "Just a little." He added hastily, "I quite like dandelions."

"It's too light," said Cossypha, shaking her head. "My head feels all funny. And cold."

"You look like a dandelion blowing in the breeze, shaking your head like that," I said, and skipped nimbly out of reach.

"You," said Cossypha, "look like a chimney sweep's brush. An old one that's lost half its bristles."

I stuck out my tongue at her. There was really nothing I could say; I did look something like that. But nobody teased Darby about his tail.

Chapter Twelve

In Which Everything Is Finished

Traditionally, the Hero is supposed to take the head away with him as a trophy, but the Dragon's head was as big as a horse so we left it with the rest of the Dragon. We took only one of its teeth to put in the Royal Treasury and Museum of Erythroth.

"They can send a Scientific Expedition to get the rest if they want," said Rufik, and that is in fact what happened. The skeleton of the Dragon was mounted on display in a new wing of the Museum, with a bronze plaque telling how Prince Rufik and Lady Cossypha the

Enchantress had saved the kingdom. It didn't say anything about me, because nobody but Rufik and Cossypha knew about me. But years later, after Rufik became king, he carved, *and Torrie too*, on the plaque, and it was a mystery to historians ever afterwards. But that's all later, like I said.

We travelled south for a week before we came to the lands near the capital city on the seacoast, and then suddenly we were there. The air was salt-tasting and the wind whipped around us sounding like a storm, although it was a bright and sunny day.

"Ah," said Rufik. "A nice calm day."

"This is calm?" Cossypha asked.

"You don't get real winds up in your mountains," said Rufik, and grinned happily. "Come on, I'll race you."

I shrieked as the horses took off, and clutched Cossypha's waist. She had no hair to hang on to any more. We pounded along the road leaving a trail of red dust to blow over the fields.

"Hey!" I shouted over the noise of the hooves and the jingling harness and the wind. "There are farmers here!" They were the first people we had seen in days.

"Of course!" Rufik called back over his shoulder. "The city is over this hill."

The men and women in the fields looked up as they heard the horses pounding on the red road. They waved and pointed.

"It's the Crown Prince!" I heard one woman cry as we whirled by. The horses pulling the hay wagons whinnied after us, and a man on top of one waved a pitchfork.

"The Dragon must be dead!"

"Prince Rufik has slain the Dragon!"

We galloped up to where the road rolled over the hill and Banner reared up, neighing.

"Look Cossy!" cried Rufik. "The city!"

Cossypha rode Darby in circles around Banner until he calmed down.

"You're fast!" he said to Banner. She just chuckled.

"It's beautiful," said Cossypha, and it was. The city wall was white, and all the houses were built of white and grey stone, and the roofs were bright copper and green. The tall towers of the castle looked out over the white-flecked sea, and the red and gold Hound of Erythroth flew over the battlements. There were many, many ships in port, flying the royal banner as well. The navy was ready to take the citizens away to safety if the Dragon came.

The people who had been working in the fields caught up with us there and crowded around, suddenly too shy to say anything to their Prince.

Finally one young boy spoke up. "Is…is the Dragon dead, Your Highness?"

"Very dead," said Rufik gravely.

"Did you kill it, sir?" asked a man. "You found the

Sword and killed the Dragon?"

"I did," said Rufik. "With a great deal of help. Allow me to present the Lady Cossypha, who is going to become my wife."

"Oh, Your Highness, how wonderful," said an old woman, and they all bowed and curtsied to Cossy, who blushed and looked shy.

"I think tomorrow we will have a celebration in the city," said Rufik. "But now, I must go and see my father."

We rode down toward the city, while the farmers hurried off to tell their neighbours that the Prince had returned victorious.

"You didn't ask," said Cossypha.

"Ask what?" asked Rufik, who was eager to get to the city and was not paying attention.

"You didn't ask if I would marry you."

"Didn't I?" asked the Prince in surprise. "I thought I had."

"No, you didn't."

"Oh," he said. "I'm sorry. Would you, Cossypha?"

"Of course she will," I said. "Really, Rufik, that's a silly thing to ask. Why else do you think we stole you from Sporryl and ran away with you?"

"That is not why," said Cossypha sternly. "Be quiet, Torrie."

"It is so why," I said. "It was my great plan."

"Torrie!" said Cossypha so severely that I squeaked

and jumped over to hide behind Rufik.

"You can't expect him to propose if you interrupt," said Banner.

"But he knows she'll marry him," I said. "And she knows it, and Darby knows it, and you and I both know it, so why bother? It's all working out like I planned from the first."

"Because a lady likes to be asked these things properly," said Banner, and swished her tail. "Right Darby?"

"I don't know anything about it," said Darby, looking like he was trying not to remember how silly his own tail looked at the moment.

"Banner says you have to ask her properly," I whispered to Rufik.

"Well, if that's how it's done," said Rufik, and he flung himself off the horse and knelt down in the road. Darby almost walked on him.

"Lady Cossypha," said Rufik grandly, "if you don't marry me, the sun will seem dark, and the moon will be dull, and winter will not sparkle, and spring will be bitter—ask Banner if that's good enough, Torrie—and I will be awfully miserable for the rest of my life."

"Of course," said Cossypha. "After all, it's Torrie's plan."

And they both laughed. At me.

"There's someone coming," I said. "It's a little round man and a little round woman and they're riding little round white ponies."

"Those," said Rufik, "are my parents, the King and Queen of Erythroth."

And so they were.

We had a tremendous feast that night, even me, although the King and Queen and all the court could not see me, and then we had hot baths all round and went to bed early, so we wouldn't be too tired for the celebration the next day. All the populace came to the city, and people danced and sang in the streets all day, and the King announced that the Dragon was officially slain and his son the Crown Prince Rufik James Augustus was going to marry the Lady Cossypha. And then the people who had fled from the Dragon to the city packed up all their belongings in carts and went home to harvest the grain. There were long parades of cows and sheep on all the highways for several days.

The plump little Queen was so delighted that her son had found such a beautiful bride, rather than being eaten by the Dragon which was what she thought would happen, that she took charge of Cossypha at once, and found jewels for her in the treasury, and set about having dresses made, and satin slippers, and silk scarves, and all the other things a Lady needs when she is going to balls in between adventures. And of course, she needed a wedding dress. So poor Cossy spent a great deal of time every day standing around on a chair while a flock of ladies tried this colour and that with her hair, and pinned lengths of white and silver silk around her and sometimes to her by accident, and Rufik was beset by tailors doing the same thing to him, and the horses and I grew back our fur. Even Darby's tail grew, eventually.

"What about Sporryl the Enchanter?" asked Bobbin. "What happened to him? I bet you've forgotten all about him."

"If you listen, you'll find out," said Torrie. "And I never forget anything."

The day of the wedding came. The whole city was decked with flowers, the streets were strewn with them, and little children ran around throwing roses at everybody, getting in practice for when the bride rode by. They were going to ride in procession to the cathedral, and Darby was even vainer than ever, now that his tail was hairy again and braided with roses and lilies. Just when we were ready to start (I had decided to ride behind Rufik, because Cossypha's long veil, silk lace and pearls had already gotten tangled up with me on the stairs), a small group of people rode into the courtyard, unchallenged by the guard. They were led by an old man with long white hair who was riding a piebald mare.

"Excuse me," he said, very politely, to the Prime Minister, who had gone to investigate. "But I believe my daughter is here."

"Your daughter?" asked the Prime Minister, raising an eyebrow curiously.

"Yes," said the man, looking around him. "She's being married today. We had a tremendous ride to get here in time."

"I don't believe I know you," said the Prime Minister, rather severely. He had organized the Wedding Procession, and seemed to feel that unannounced old men with white hair and purple robes were not supposed to be part of it.

"Oh," said the old man. "I'm Sporryl the Enchanter, of course. Cossypha's father."

"Aha!" said Bobbin.
"Quiet," said the toad.

It had never occurred to the Prime Minister that Lady Cossypha had a father at all, but all was sorted out by the Court Poet, who stood up in his stirrups and hollered, "Milady Cossypha!" across the crowded courtyard.

"Father!" shrieked Cossypha, and flew across the yard with her long veil streaming behind her.

"Hello dear," said Sporryl. Dear! he called her. "I hear

you've killed a dragon and met a prince."

"I met him in your dungeon," said Cossypha, a little severely, but not very.

"Well, yes," said Sporryl. "But really, that's all over now. No hard feelings, young man? I don't believe we've been introduced."

Cossypha introduced Rufik to her father, and they shook hands. Sporryl hardly looked like the same man when he was smiling. And he winked at me! He saw me! He must have known about me all along! I felt all weak and wobbly and had to sit down.

The Court Poet was busily introducing everybody to everybody else, he was so excited he even introduced Rufik to Cossypha. Sporryl's cook, who had been a rather plump wolf guard, and the two kitchen maids, who had been skinny wolf guards, hurried off to help the king's kitchen staff put the final touches on the wedding banquet, and the rest of us prepared to start for the cathedral.

Sporryl helped his daughter gracefully into the saddle, and the Queen arranged her veil, and the King slapped the Court Poet on the shoulder and said wasn't it wonderful, and Rufik, wearing Wormbane, looked noble and princely and couldn't take his eyes off Cossy. Sporryl stood looking at Cossypha for a minute; then, with a shy little smile, he handed her a bouquet of roses out of the air. The most wonderful, amazing roses they were; their scent filled the courtyard and blue butterflies fluttered around them.

Cossypha leaned down and kissed his cheek and everybody cheered heartily, and the Prime Minister scurried frantically around getting the procession in its proper order. Cossy threw me a rose when no one was looking.

Sporryl came over and shook Rufik's hand again, and chuckled at me, sitting half under Rufik's crimson cloak where he might not see me.

"Come on, Torrie," said the Enchanter. "You can ride with me. I want to hear what happened to Cossypha's hair."

And they were married, and everybody lived happily ever after.

The gingery bear sighed happily. "That's how a story should end."

"Is that the end already?" asked the deer-footed imp.

"It's the end of this story," said Torrie.

"Weren't there any more goblins?" asked Bobbin.

"None whatsoever," said Torrie. "At least not then."

"Tell me some more about the goblins."

"There were no more goblins," said Torrie sternly.

"Oh," said Bobbin. "Well, did Cossypha's father stay a good Enchanter forever, or did he go back to being evil again?"

"He was a good Enchanter for the rest of his life."

"Did any more adventures happen to Rufik and Cossypha?" the purple toad-thing asked.

"Maybe," said Torrie. "Maybe not."

"Will you tell them to us?" asked the toad-thing. "Tonight?"

"Maybe someday," Torrie said. "Not tonight."

"Why not?" asked Bobbin.

"Because it's morning," said Torrie, and laughed. "Look."

The sun was coming up, turning the birch trees pink. The gingery bear yawned.

"I can show you a trick Sporryl taught me, though," said Torrie. "Watch."

He whispered a word and struck the embers of the bonfire with his spear. There was a puff of smoke and a burst of purple flame. The fire went out. And Torrie had disappeared. From somewhere down in the woods, Bobbin thought she heard him giggling, but she wasn't sure.

In ones and twos, the animals and the Old Things of the Wild Forest slipped away, until the top of the hill was deserted save for the ashes of the bonfire and one robin, starting to sing.

About the Author

K.V. Johansen is a Mediævalist by training, with a B.A. in English from Mount Allison University, an M.A. from the Centre for Medieval Studies at the University of Toronto, and a second Masters degree, in English, from McMaster University. She is a regular contributor to various magazines, and currently resides in rural New Brunswick. *Torrie and the Dragon* is her first Middle Reader.

AGMV
MARQUIS
Québec, Canada
1997